Sign Language for "Please Come In!"

Faro chuckled suddenly. "My dad used to tell me that the best secret is one that everybody knows already, but nobody can do."

Evelyn Sutcliff threw back her head and laughed, setting the top from of her gown to rippling in a way that impressed Faro mightily. He had been pretty sure that she wasn't whaleboned up under the gown, but the laugh made the matter clear. She said, "That's so true of so many things, isn't it? There are things you know, but you can't reveal them—and awfully few people can do them, right?"

"What kinds of things, ma'am?" Faro asked, leaning back, amused. Funny how some women seemed to have to make a whole vaudeville act out of this stuff—the polite conversation and so on—all leading up to where they just about were now. Mrs. S. was horny and had roped him out of the herd for the job, and there it was.

"Things it doesn't do to *talk* about," she said with mock primness.

She refilled their brandy glasses, leaning closer to him, bringing the scent of her perfume and a sharper musky odor closer and closer. . . .

Books by Zeke Masters

The Big Gamble
Diamond Flush
Luck of the Draw
Threes Are Wild

Published by POCKET BOOKS

#4

A ZEKE MASTERS WESTERN

DIAMOND FLUSH

PUBLISHED BY POCKET BOOKS NEW YORK

Another *Original* publication of POCKET BOOKS

POCKET BOOKS, a Simon & Schuster division of
GULF & WESTERN CORPORATION
1230 Avenue of the Americas, New York, N.Y. 10020

ISBN: 0–671–83435–5

First Pocket Books printing October, 1980

10 9 8 7 6 5 4 3 2 1

POCKET and colophon are trademarks of Simon & Schuster.

Printed in the U.S.A.

DIAMOND FLUSH

Chapter 1

Honeytown, Kansas, was just the sort of place Faro Blake had hoped it would be. Wide open and roaring. Immediately on his arrival—courtesy of the Atchison, Topeka & Santa Fe Railroad—he checked into the Chicago House. Finding that the bank was closed until two o'clock, he decided to take a walk and check out business prospects. The town certainly offered a multitude of gambling establishments, as "You Lose" Lewis had promised. The question for Faro was, which was the best. It was high noon as he found himself standing at the long bar in Honeytown's most populated and most lucrative saloon, the Goldroom.

The Goldroom was large, lively and famous along the Kansas–Indian Territory border. Like most of Honeytown's gambling and drinking establishments, it operated twenty-four hours a day. Faro noted five monte tables, two wheels of fortune, several tables for poker, dice, and in fact just about any gambling activity. He stood with his back to the room, leaning on the bar, taking in the action through the big wall mirror in front of him. The mahogany bar, brought all the way from Wichita, ran almost the length of the room. Besides the gaming tables there were chairs lining the far wall on which nonplaying clientele relaxed and occasionally conversed on such various importances as the weather, the Texas cattle quarantine, the fortunes of dice, cards, horse racing and badger fighting, or the merits of the "soiled doves" who adroitly plied their trade in the three houses in the raunchy community known as "Hide Park."

Faro was just pondering whether he would approach Homer Tyng, the proprietor of the Goldroom, about opening a faro bank or wait until he had checked some of the other establishments when an enormous man barged through the batwing doors.

"Well, if it ain't Horrible McCluskie himself in person," muttered the man standing next to Faro. He was talking to no one in particular it seemed. Like Faro, he had his back to the room and was viewing the new arrival in the mirror. He was a thin, unhealthy looking individual with a loose, wet mouth and whining eyes. Faro had heard him referred to by the name Cherokee Dan. He was drunk.

Faro turned now to face the approaching McCluskie and suddenly, as he observed the big man's nimble gait, his thick gorselike mustache, swooping like the horns on a longhorn steer, he felt a lift of recognition. Of course!

Horrible Henry McCluskie, one of those cow-town characters of whom he had heard, though never actually met, was a self-styled Wild Bill Hickok with gold earrings, a fancy vest, and, Faro had not failed to notice, a brace of side arms. Faro wondered how Horrible McCluskie managed to ignore the large signs about town prohibiting firearms, when he saw the star on the brocaded vest.

Horrible Henry had just reached the bar where Faro was standing when Cherokee Dan turned suddenly and spoke.

"How's about setting 'em up for the boys, McCluskie?"

Something in the man's voice caught Faro and he felt himself stiffen. There was definitely something wrong with the way Cherokee Dan had said the words.

Horrible McCluskie must have noticed also, for without breaking stride, without even a glance at the man beside Faro, he said, "You can go piss up a rope, you mangy little sonofabitch!"

Faro saw the color whip into the other man's face while he involuntarily took a step forward as though he had been struck. And it was clear to Faro how much he had been drinking, for he all but staggered.

Without further ado, Horrible Henry McClus-kie drove his enormous fist into Cherokee Dan's neck, and as the man began to fall, smashed him again along the side of his head.

Faro wondered if maybe the blows had been mortal; but liquor again proved its worth in a crisis. Dan was as limp as a sack of old laundry. He spilled to the floor, but almost immediately began struggling to his feet. His hand gripped the edge of a spittoon for support and upset its contents on his arm. He began slowly and painfully to pull himself up onto the bar, and now lay gasping against it.

Hardly anyone in the room appeared to notice the altercation, save for some of those worthies tilting their chairs against the wall. But Faro reminded himself that this was Honeytown, the Border Queen, the toughest of the cowtowns in the 1870s, and such matters were run-of-the-mill.

McCluskie waited while Cherokee Dan tried to gain his breath, supporting himself on the bar. The lawman was holding a glass of whiskey in his left hand, while his right stayed close to one of his holstered six-guns. Dan had clearly had enough for the evening; finally, he turned and staggered to the door of the saloon—his breath sawing, his head bent to his shoulder—and disappeared, with only three or four heads marking his passage.

"Deputy Marshal Henry McCluskie, stranger," the huge man said, turning to Faro.

"Faro Blake."

"Just arrived in our happy town, have ya?" McCluskie's air was engaging, and Faro couldn't help but smile.

"Just in time for the festivities," he said wryly. And at that, Horrible McCluskie boomed out with laughter. "And it's all free, Faro Blake; all for free!" He roared, wiping his eyes with a thick knuckle. Faro was about to spring for a round of drinks as he watched the deputy's big belly push against the bar, causing a button to pop off and fall into his glass with a little click.

"Aw shit," said Horrible McCluskie. But he

was not speaking about the button. He was speaking about Cherokee Dan whom, Faro could now see through the mirror, was standing in the doorway of the Goldroom.

This time Dan's presence did attract attention. Cherokee's head was bent almost to his shoulder, his face was a mask of pain, and he was wearing a holstered six-gun. His mouth was working as he stared at McCluskie, and now he tried to lift his arm so that he could draw.

Faro's immediate impulse was to step in right there and stop it, for the man was helpless and no match for the deputy. But he was a stranger in town, and this was none of his business. So, he did nothing as Horrible Henry McCluskie drew one of his big Navy Colts and fired. Unaccountably at that close range, the first bullet missed. But the second drilled right into Cherokee Dan's head.

Nobody had to say it, but someone did.

"He's dead." It was the bartender who pronounced those words, while standing a good twenty feet away from the fresh corpse, and wiping his hands on his apron.

Seeing that the big wall clock pointed to two o'clock, Faro decided it was time to get on to the bank and make his deposit. Nodding to McCluskie, who was calmly sipping his whiskey, he took his departure. As he went out the door, the bartender and a man who had been sitting against the wall took hold of the late Cherokee Dan.

The bank was at the corner of Main and Fifth streets, a one-story building with a large window on which gold letters proclaimed it Bank of Honeytown, Kansas.

"I'd like to see the manager," Faro said to the teller, a crisp young man with a short mustache and a very clean blue shirt.

"Do you wish to make a deposit, sir?"

Faro stopped then. Reaching into his coat pocket he drew out a cigar. He took his time lighting it. Then he said, "I think I said I want to see the manager, mister."

"Is there something I can do?" a soft, musical voice suddenly cut in before the confused teller could speak.

Faro turned to face a tall, blond, rather ravishing creature. His irritation fled on the spot, and a smile broke over his wide, angular face. She was probably in her early thirties, he judged, and her cobalt blue eyes turned up at the corners.

"I am certain I could find something, ma'am," he said, deepening his Kentucky drawl and keeping his green eyes fully upon her.

"I am the manager, sir." The voice was friendly, but by no means bantering as his had been, and Faro was brought up short.

He was stone-serious as he said, "I want to make a deposit."

"George can handle that, I am quite sure. . . ."

"It's a rather large deposit," Faro said. "Twenty thousand dollars."

"I see. Will you come to my office, Mister—?"

"Blake. Faro Blake."

"I am Evelyn Sutcliff."

Faro bent to the proffered hand in true Kentucky style. And as he followed her into her office, his eyes played agreeably along the lines of her moving haunches. Evelyn Sutcliff, he assured himself, was clearly all delight.

The actual business was transacted in only a few minutes, while at the same time Mrs. Sutcliff informed him that she had taken over the bank on the death of her husband a year ago. She announced that she was more than ready to come out of mourning, and Faro felt only too ready to help her celebrate her return to the good things of life.

The next day, the victim of Horrible Henry McCluskie's accuracy was buried. The marshal was out of town chasing bandits who had held up the stage to Thornburgh, and nobody wanted to arrest McCluskie. But the citizens and Town Council insisted a trial should take place immediately, the point being that a fresh herd of Texas cattle was due any day now, and it was sensible to get such business as the killing out of the way before the town was stampeded by Texans. Another point was that Finn Tolliver was passing through and since he had "taken law back East," he would be suitable to officiate on the bench. Happily, the problem of the arrest of Deputy McCluskie was settled by the Horrible one giving himself up. "I got no reason not to," he put it. "It was clear self-defense. So let's get on with it."

Faro did not attend Cherokee Dan's funeral, but that afternoon he did come to the trial. This turned out to be a notable event, and Faro was pleased that he had decided to attend. It was his abiding passion to study people—a trait he had clearly picked up from his gambling father, Aaron Burr Blake, back in the riverboat days when A.B. had been teaching him the trade.

There being no courthouse in Honeytown, Cal

Canton had offered his Do-Drop Saloon for the afternoon. A seat was provided for Finn Tolliver, and another for McCluskie. A table was placed between them. In the event anybody got thirsty, a pitcher of water and a large pitcher of whiskey were set on the table. Tolliver, as judge and also as prosecutor, opened the proceedings by sampling the libation offered by Cal Canton.

The trial had hardly started when a brisk difference of opinion broke out. Horrible McCluskie had taken a large cigar out of his pocket, offered one to Finn Tolliver, and when both men lit up a juror protested.

"With a man on trial for his life," the juror said, "it don't seem fittin' for you two fellers to be smokin'."

A lively debate followed, spurred by various draughts of whiskey and not so much water. But at length Tolliver handed down a ruling.

"Since it is a trial for the defendant's life, and since he might lose his life, then there ain't no reason he shouldn't enjoy one or two of the good things of this here life before going either up or down."

The soundness of this argument impressed all, and as a consequence, many lit up. The trial proceeded.

A parade of witnesses moved to the stand, some slightly worse for visits to the pitcher of whiskey. Faro enjoyed it hugely, and since he was not on duty at the moment, he too sampled Cal Canton's pitcher. It was surely a sensible way to conduct a trial for a man's life.

The course of the trial was slow, and while there was little dispute as to what had occurred, recesses had to be called while the pitcher of brown fluid was replenished.

Finn Tolliver, a tall, thin man with a long, bony jaw, deep-socketed eyes and a stoop—the result of having long ago been tromped by a bronc—now stood up and faced the jury. Faro could see he was quite unsteady on his pins, but no less loquacious for that fact as he opened the prosecution's concluding argument.

"I object!" roared Horrible McCluskie before Tolliver had finished his first paragraph.

"On what grounds?" demanded Finn Tolliver, glowering down upon the defendant.

"I'm sayin' ain't you the judge?" roared Mc-Cluskie.

Finn Tolliver was unmoved by the outburst. With the finality of an undertaker he said, "Yes, and I am also the prosecutor. Objection over-ruled."

He continued his argument, pleading elo-quently for conviction and the extreme penalty. Horrible McCluskie listened passively with a smile on his face. Faro could see how he was enjoying himself. After all, the liquor was agree-able, and there was plenty of it.

Finn Tolliver finally finished and sat down.

"Is that pitcher empty?" a juror demanded.

All eyes turned sadly to the pitcher which someone opined was "drier'n a bull's ass in fly time."

"I move we hang him," someone said.

"We ought to hang him," a second juror agreed.

"He did kill Cherokee Dan."

"And he finished the whiskey."

"There's more whiskey," Cal Canton said, "but we better decide on this."

"We better get that whiskey."

"Let's hang him first."

Finn Tolliver said, "We got to hear the other side. I ain't pronounced on Horrible yet. We got to hear the defense, and then when he's guilty we hang him."

There was a disgruntled murmur of approval at this, and a stirring of feet and scraping of chairs as Horrible Henry McCluskie stood up.

"Who you got for defending lawyer?" Finn Tolliver asked.

"I'm defending myself," Henry said.

"Shoot."

"Thing is, I admit to shooting Cherokee Dan, but I didn't kill him."

There was a great murmur from the jurors at this. "What the hell d'ya mean?"

"Cherokee was scared shitless of me. You agree on that?"

"Sure do," said a juror. "He was scared of everybody, but 'specially you."

"An' he was a weak man. You agree?"

Horrible McCluskie had their interest now, and they were all hanging on his words. Faro too was wondering what the deputy was going to come up with.

"And you agree his health wasn't none too good."

A wave of approval swept the room. Finn Tolliver was glaring, but he had to go along. Anyhow, Cal Canton had refilled the whiskey pitcher.

"Then," said McCluskie, raising his forefinger high in the air, "I says this. I says Cherokee Dan didn't die of gunshot, but he was just plumb scared to death. He died, I'm sayin', of a heart attack *before* my bullet hit him!"

A stunned silence fell upon the group. No one even made a move toward the pitcher of whiskey.

The silence lengthened until at last Finn Tolliver rose to his feet. Horrible McCluskie had long since collapsed into his chair.

"Hell," Tolliver said, "we can't hang him tonight anyways. I'm for callin' a mistrial. Shit, there ain't a one of us sober enough to tie the fuckin' hanging knot."

At this the courtroom erupted in agreement. Horrible McCluskie rose and waving his arms over his head bellowed his grateful thanks to the judge and jurors. "I just knowed justice would triumph," he said.

"Amen," Finn Tolliver said, sitting down and closing his eyes. In a moment he was fast asleep.

Yes, Faro decided as he walked out into the early evening air. Honeytown was the town for him. It was for sure a town with a sense of humor, and you couldn't ask much more than that.

Chapter 2

"Honeytown, hell!" said one old-timer. "It's more Honey Dip is what they are meanin'!"

Whether or not it was outhouse "honey" as the old-timer suggested, Faro still liked it. Hughie Lewis had been right when he'd urged him to go there. That had been down in San Antonio when Hughie had said:

"During cattle season the money rolls in quicker'n a cat can lick his ass. Big money, I say. Herds comin' up from Texas and bein' sold right now; trail crews and owners just lookin' to get rid of their money."

Hughie "You Lose" Lewis's eyes opened big as silver dollars. "I mean, Faro, it's a gambling paradise. And I'm tellin' you the straight of it. When I sell my critters off, if you be there in Honeytown, I'll be playing my roll agin yourn for the whole of it, by God!"

Faro smiled to himself thinking of "You Lose" Lewis, a wealthy Texas rancher who had lost heavily, especially to Faro, in the mammoth poker game in Santone the previous July.

"Justifyin' his nickname," someone had said after the event. But "You Lose" had the born gambler's lust to continue high-stakes play, and Faro had accepted both his advice and challenge. So he was here in Honeytown, the new Border Queen, at the height of the season.

Less than a year earlier the Atchison, Topeka & Santa Fe Railroad had completed a line of track to what was then only the town site. Stockyards were swiftly erected. The first building, which happened to be a blacksmith shop, was moved there from Cherryville, and the first hotel—the Chicago House—was built. Other business houses and homes were put up at a tremendous rate. The town was still singing to the sound of saw and hammer when Faro got there; to say nothing of the bawling of cattle and the crash of gunfire from high-jinxing cowboys. True, there was the law against carrying firearms in town, but then there was also the law against drinking in the streets and a lot of other things.

Honeytown, on the border of the Indian Territory, had a regular population of from twelve to fifteen hundred. The town was all wood save for the depot, which was plastered. The sidewalks on Main Street were ten feet wide and made of wood. The streets were still covered with grass. Only a few days before Faro's arrival at Honeytown, the Town Council had passed an ordinance prohibiting buffaloes and other wild animals from running at large in the town's streets.

Faro was happy to see so many saloons and gambling halls. There were in fact twenty-nine places in Honeytown where liquor was served, and a dozen gambling shops dealt the action. Every device invented for gambling could be found—faro banks, chuck-a-luck, hazard, monte, poker of all kinds, old sledge, the tobacco box game, wheels of fortune, dice. Each gambling establishment had a bar, and some had free lunch and concert music, the latter for the purpose of retaining clientele that would surely find a stronger magnet in the dance houses in Hide Park, where the fiddled strains of such popular tunes as "Chicken in the Breadtray" and "Old Dan Tucker," accompanied by the scraping sound of boots, could be heard at any time of day or night, including Sunday.

While alarm at the spread of tick fever carried by Texas cattle was threatening some cattle towns—with the quarantine line being pushed steadily westward—Honeytown had the advantage of being located on the border between the state of Kansas and the Indian Territory, so that should the quarantine be extended that far, the cattle holding-pens could be moved swiftly across the state line, out of Kansas jurisdiction.

As he stood outside the Goldroom just after Horrible McCluskie's trial, enjoying a fresh cigar, Faro did indeed feel he had made the right choice. Yet he cautioned himself that he must not let himself get too comfortable. A.B. had warned on that. "Son, when you start feeling you got it all figured out, that's just when you're going to get clotheslined."

He let his eyes fall to the sign posted on the

wall beside the batwing doors. It announced that Rev. C. L. Underwood of Ellenburg would preach on Sunday at the Goldroom saloon, and that immediately upon the conclusion of the services, a horse race and a badger fight were scheduled. Taking one last look at the busy street, the deep evening sky, Faro walked through the swinging doors.

Homer Tyng, the proprietor of the Goldroom, turned out to be an agreeable man. After saying how he regretted not being there when Faro had called in the day before, Tyng agreed to the arrangement whereby Faro would open his faro bank and would also deal poker.

"It's honest play at the Goldroom," Tyng said. "I have heard of your reputation for square faro-dealing."

It pleased Faro to find that his reputation had preceded him. It was decidedly good for business.

Tyng was a corpulent man, though not flabby. He seemed to draw to a point at top and bottom, somewhat like a top. He moved gracefully, as fat people sometimes do, and he had a fine sense of humor.

Signaling the bartender for a round, Homer leaned on the bar, letting a smile spread across his shiny face. "Just heard from an old friend of mine," he said. "Floyd Greenough, over to Dodge. Used to be a waddy for Burns & Kriser. About four years ago he was topping a bronc, and the animal fell on him. Floyd's foot was busted all to hell. Lucky it was only that; now he got this limp. But old man Kriser was a square one and on account of Floyd couldn't handle horses anymore—had to walk with a crutch—he let him have a kind of allowance, a pension for his foot."

The proprietor of the Goldroom paused, chuckling deep in his ample chest, and took a long draught of whiskey before going on.

"Just got a letter from old Floyd. Appears he had another accident. Some people are always havin' accidents, you know. This time he got drunk and hit by a locomotive on the Santa Fe. Lost his leg." Homer started to shake. Faro, meanwhile, was wondering what was so damn funny about getting hit by a train and losing your leg.

Homer couldn't control it. Tears sprouted from his eyes, and he dabbed helplessly at them with his fat knuckles while wheels of laughter rolled out of his gasping mouth. Finally, he managed to subside sufficiently to say, "You don't see what's so funny, do ya, Blake."

"Can't say I do, Homer." But Faro couldn't help laughing along with the contagious fat man.

"Thing is," Tyng said, still gasping, "thing is, the leg was the one that had the mangled foot. So, I just got the letter like I told you . . . Floyd is all put out on account of old man Kriser stopped his pension." And as he said the words, Homer burst into a fresh crescendo of laughter.

"You get it, do ya? You get it? Old Kriser figgers Floyd don't have that busted up foot anymore."

Homer Tyng finally moved away, on a signal from one of his bartenders, but still chortled over his friend Floyd's mishap.

"Homer's a square shooter," a voice said at

Faro's elbow. And turning, he found himself looking across the bar into the cleft between two superb half-naked breasts. These, he soon discovered, were supported by a firm body and legs topped by wickedly laughing hazel eyes. It was the bartender for the late-night shift who owned all this delicious flesh and muscle. Faro's estimation of Homer Tyng's business acumen rose considerably.

"He may be square, Miss, but he sure knows how to decorate this place," Faro said.

"Glad you like it." As she ran a rag across the top of the bar, she leaned forward so that Faro had an even better view.

"You have a name?" Faro asked.

"Janey Hand."

"I'm Faro Blake."

"I've heard about you."

"I've heard of you, too."

At this she showed surprise. "You have?"

Faro laughed, showing to advantage his fine white teeth, while the urge to get closer to her grew rapidly stronger.

"I have known you in my dreams," he said, and he looked directly into her eyes.

At this point a customer called for drinks, and the girl moved away, leaving behind her a strong scent of perfume which Faro found particularly exciting.

Thank you for sex, he was thinking. God, was there anything else even half as good? And he remembered A.B. telling him, "Sonny boy, just don't ever forget that sex is the most fun you can have without laughing."

Faro knew he never would.

Chapter 3

It was about eight o'clock in the evening when Faro set up his bank and made ready to play. He had already found an assistant for paying and collecting the bets, and also a casekeeper to manipulate the small box that contained a miniature layout with four buttons running along a steel rod opposite each card. It was his job to move the buttons along, as on a billiard counter, as the cards were played, so that the players could immediately tell what cards remained to be dealt. With care Faro placed his layout, the suit of thirteen cards, all spades, painted on a large square of enameled oilcloth. The cards on the layout were arranged in two parallel rows, with the ace on the dealer's left and the odd card, the seven, on his extreme right. There was ample space between the rows for the players to place their bets. In the row nearest the players were the king, queen, and jack, called the "big figure," and the ten, nine and eight. In the row nearest the dealer were the ace, deuce, and trey, the "little figure," and the four, five and six. The six, seven and eight were called the "pot." The king, queen, ace and deuce were called the "grand square"; the jack, three, four and ten were the "jack square," and the nine, eight, six and five were the "nine square."

The Goldroom was thick with customers, tobacco smoke and the smell of men as Faro shuffled and cut the cards, and then placed them face upward in the dealing box, the top of which was, of course, open.

In the hands of an honest dealer, faro was considered the fairest banking game ever devised. In no other game was the percentage against the player so small. In fact, with the first and last cards dead, the bank had no advantage at all except what might be found in the splits, and this was so slight as to make the game almost pure chance.

And Faro, over the years, continued to take pride in sticking to his principle of dealing square faro. Trim a sucker at poker or dice or any other game; but the bank was another matter. Of course, he would never have admitted to such sentiments. Once, when asked why he insisted on always dealing honest faro, he had simply replied, "Habit."

True, Faro loved to win, but his main pleasure was always the game, no matter whether it was cards, horse racing or betting on how many years someone had worn a beard. The game and the people who played.

Thus, Faro was vastly amused to discover that

Horrible Henry McCluskie was still on the payroll as deputy marshal. The killing of Cherokee Dan was simply accepted as a minor event. For sure, Cherokee had indeed tried to draw on Horrible. And he would certainly have shot *him* if he could have. And maybe he *had* died of a heart attack. No sawbones in the community had volunteered to perform an autopsy, and the incident was closed. The ill-feeling that had led up to the shooting, the reason for Horrible Henry beating Dan with his fists in the first place, was unknown.

Faro had been standing at the bar in the Goldroom a couple of days after the event when a drummer who had witnessed the action had asked Jake the bartender about it. Faro found the answer impressive in its poetic simplicity.

To the question "Why did McCluskie kill Cherokee Dan; what reason did he have?" the man behind the bar replied:

"Horrible didn't like Dan."

That evening it was warm in the Goldroom. No one thought to open any windows to allow air to enter. Gambling folk for some reason always liked old air and used atmospheres. And Faro shared the preference. He was not a man for the open spaces and would have felt uncomfortable working in full daylight and fresh air.

He had been dealing faro just a couple of hours, breaking even, when he heard rather than saw Horrible Henry McCluskie walk in. Faro was busy watching his casekeeper, an able operator, and he continued to keep his eyes on him while feeling the approach of McCluskie. The big man was now standing directly in front of him, his breath wheezing out a combination of tobacco, garlic and rotten teeth so powerful that Faro winced.

"Like a word with you, Blake." The words were grunted, along with a liberal dose of breath.

"Sure enough," Faro said, while finishing up the play. McCluskie was still wearing the two Navy Colts and he stood swing-hipped with his thumbs hooked into his big, wide belt.

"That will do for now, gentlemen," Faro said. And with a nod to his casekeeper he closed the bank. "The drinks are on me," he said to McCluskie as they pushed up to the bar.

Horrible Henry chuckled appreciatively at that. It sounded a bit like thunder, Faro thought; while the jovial pat on his shoulder that accompanied it was like the caress of a grizzly.

"Make it whiskey," Horrible said; sniffing loudly and wiping his big red nose along the back of his hairy hand. He chuckled again. "I be needin' a trim. This here mustache likes to tickle my nose; makes me sneeze." And even as he said it, his face suddenly reddened, his eyes squinted, tears appeared and as he drew back his big head Faro dodged for cover. The roar of Horrible McCluskie's sneeze shook the room.

Faro returned to the bar, glad that the drinks had not yet been served. At least his bourbon had not been flavored.

Faro's reaction amused McCluskie. "Sometimes it rains," he said, starting to chuckle, "and sometimes it roars!" And he let out a roar of laughter at his joke.

Faro was wondering what it was all leading to, but he remained patient, simply waiting for the other to show his hand. He watched in admiration as Horrible downed two whiskeys in rapid succession and pushed his glass forward for a refill. Faro obliged, helping himself to another as well. Turning toward him now, the big man leaned against the bar like a great tree.

"Figgered it was due me to educate you a bit, Blake, bein' as how you are a stranger in this here town." A big smile broke agreeably over the whole of his face, and brown stumps suddenly appeared under his mustache. Faro knew now what was coming and he couldn't help smiling to himself. McCluskie was likable, no about about that, and human beings were surely greedy. Had it ever been otherwise?

"Let 'er rip," he said.

"See, I'm special constable here in Honeytown—under Cole, of course. Cole Herkimer that is, the marshal. You probably ain't run into him yet on account of he is out chasin' the stage bandits. Well, we are the law here. And so I got to inform you that there is a tax on your operation."

"My operation?" Faro decided to play it absolutely innocent. As he spoke he noticed a tall man moving up to the bar just behind McCluskie.

"Your bank. Gambling. Gamblers got to pay a tax," Horrible explained.

"How much?"

McCluskie pursed his lips fast, squinted, and then said immediately, "Five percent of your gross betting on any game you run."

"Five percent!"

Horrible McCluskie held up a huge paw to forestall any more objection. "It's the law."

Faro, meanwhile, had taken a cigar out of his pocket and was lighting it.

"Got another of them have ya?"

Wryly, Faro handed the deputy one of his special cigars which he had bought in Denver. "That's a pretty stiff percentage, Henry," he said. "You know, I run an honest game, and in straight faro the house percentage is well under three, and can be less. So what's that mean?" He spread his hands in an offering gesture. "It means you are asking me either to cheat or run my bank at a loss."

McCluskie's enormous shoulders raised and lowered in a shrug. The smile was not so soft now as he said, "Mister, that is tough titty."

Faro's eyes fell to the star on McCluskie's vest. The law all right, and there it was. Swiftly he had gone over the options: cheating, accepting a loss or simply not opening a faro bank. None of them appealed to him. Frankly, he liked dealing faro. He liked it a lot. At the same time, it would be idiocy simply to continue to play at a guaranteed loss. That left cheating, which was out of the question. No, faro was his trademark, and honest faro was the principle he had lived by; he wasn't going to stop now. The only way out was to get out of Honeytown.

It was just at this point that the tall man standing next to McCluskie, but unseen by the giant, suddenly moved closer. Faro got a full view of height, rectitude, a trim brown mustache and the coldest blue eyes he had ever seen. Faro realized now that he must have been listening to the conversation. As the man's hand brushed the skirt of his broadcloth coat, drawing it back slightly, Faro caught sight of the six-gun and the marshal's badge.

The voice behind all that fine clothing and armament was deep, cultured, careful. "Mister McCluskie has misinformed you, stranger." And at the words Horrible Henry whirled, almost knocking over his drink, his big face falling apart in surprise.

"Hell, I didn't know you was there behind me, Cole."

"That is evident." The words were acid. "And it is also evident, McCluskie, that you are no longer a deputy marshal in Honeytown." Cole Herkimer's hand moved imperceptibly, so that it was very close to his holstered weapon. "You may put your badge on the bar."

"Hell, Cole . . . Marshal—"

Marshal Cole Herkimer stood tall and silent, like a milled board, Faro thought. He was not giving anything.

"Shit, take it!" McCluskie roared suddenly, and he ripped off the badge and slammed it on top of the bar. Spitting furiously all over the spittoon at Faro's feet, he strode out of the room.

Faro had been looking for a fight right on the spot, but it was clear that Herkimer was no man to mess with, and even McCluskie realized that. McCluskie, Faro saw, was afraid of the marshal.

So furious was Horrible as he stormed from the room that he almost knocked down a man who was entering. But he didn't stop, he didn't pause; he just fumed out into the night.

"The name is Cole Herkimer." And the marshal offered Faro a grip that was firm, while keeping his eyes easily on the gambler; but there was nothing casual in them.

"Faro Blake."

"Straight gamblers don't have to pay protection in Honeytown, Blake. And the other kind I run out fast."

"Good to hear that, Marshal."

"Honeytown, as you can see, is wide open. Anything goes except gunplay and cheating. You know how it is—I don't have to tell a man of your obvious experience—with the cattle money coming in and begging to be spent, there'd be as much chance of enforcing laws against gambling, drinking and whoring as a fart has in a windstorm: straight games, honest drinks and clean girls are the rule in Honeytown."

"Good enough," Faro said, grinning. "Can I buy you one?"

The marshal stood away from the bar. "Next time. I must make my rounds." And with a brisk nod the tall, immaculately dressed marshal of Honeytown took his departure.

Faro ordered another bourbon. He found it interesting that Horrible McCluskie could kill a man and get away with it, but that he couldn't get away with a simple shakedown, which in fact was the order of the day in the gambling world. In most towns, if not all, he knew that the policemen received their pay from a fund raised by the gamblers. This was the tribute the gamblers had to pay for their gambling privileges. On the other hand, the keeper of a saloon obtained his license from the county, for which he paid $150. But to make payment to the fund and to McCluskie as well was bending a good thing a little too far, Faro reasoned. That sonofabitch, he thought. He was pleased to find Herkimer was straight.

For a moment he considered opening his faro bank again, but decided he could certainly profit better by getting into a few hands of poker. He ambled over to a table where there was a game in progress. Along with a number of hangers-on, Faro watched the action. What he was really doing, of course, was studying very carefully each of the players.

It was about midnight when someone left the table and Faro joined the game.

There were six players at the table besides himself, but there hadn't been much spirit in the game. Faro, of course, had a good idea of the players by now, their psychologies and habits, their little giveaway moments and gestures.

The dealer was a little man with a patch over one eye, One-Eye Jacobsen by name. Picking up the new deck, he removed the joker and announced, "This is straight draw." By that Faro knew him to mean jacks or better, that the pot couldn't be opened unless the opener had at least two jacks in his hand.

One-Eye Jacobsen dealt skillfully, a diamond as large as his thumbnail sparkling on his little finger. It had not taken Faro long to see what One-Eye was up to. The thing was that whenever he was bluffing, he cleared his throat before speaking or taking a card or placing his chips.

Another man opened the pot, and One-Eye didn't stay. On the third deal Faro opened for ten dollars, the usual, on a pair of aces. He was sitting to One-Eye's right. One-Eye raised him twenty dollars. Faro stayed and drew three cards.

One-Eye's poker face turned into a wicked

smile. He cleared his throat and said, "I play these."

Faro didn't help the aces. He knew what was coming, but he didn't know how much he would bet. One-Eye glanced at Faro's chips, calculating how much he had left.

One-Eye bet fifty dollars. Faro pretended to hesitate. "I call," he said and spread his hand, face up, showing two aces. One-Eye could not conceal a look of utter disbelief.

"I'll be hornswaggled," he declared and threw his hand face down on the discards. "Didn't you know I stood pat?" he said in disgust. "How can you call a pat hand on two aces?"

Faro smiled. "It was easy," he said.

Around four in the morning a fat little drummer named Al came in.

"Take a seat," One-Eye greeted him. Fat Al smiled back good-naturedly.

There was another vacant chair now, so Faro got up from One-Eye's side and took the other seat. Faro knew that One-Eye was going to work on the drummer, and he wanted to be in a strategic position to win when he did.

Several rounds passed before his opportunity came. He was sitting to One-Eye's left, and the drummer who was going to get stripped sat to his right.

"Let's play draw," One-Eye said, picking up a new deck and again removing the joker. He dealt swiftly, his pale white hands almost transparent under the overhead lamp, the diamond flashing with each movement.

Faro passed. The next four players passed, making five in all. The drummer, the sixth

player, opened with a ten-dollar bet. One-Eye
came out with a twenty-dollar raise. Faro called.
One-Eye showed no irritation at this, though
Faro knew he hadn't planned for more than one
player to draw against him. The drummer
called, which was according to One-Eye's plan.

Faro drew one card.

"Gonna win it, are ya?" One-Eye said pleas-
antly.

Faro didn't answer. He never talked while
playing poker except to announce his bet and the
showdown.

The drummer took three cards.

One-Eye Jacobsen said, "I play these," meaning he was standing pat.

The drummer, after a quick look at his cards,
checked.

Without a moment's hesitation One-Eye bet
fifty dollars. Faro knew he must be figuring that
he, Faro, had backed in the pot and was drawing
to a straight or a flush. Faro had learned early in
his career never to risk money drawing one card
to a straight or a flush unless there was at least
six times the amount of the bet in the pot.

When One-Eye bet fifty dollars, Faro raised
him a hundred dollars. He didn't have a thing,
but One-Eye had cleared his throat, and he knew
he was bluffing again. He was sure One-Eye was
standing pat on a bust; Fat Al the drummer
didn't matter, having checked. Even if he had
helped his hand he would hesitate to call, with
Faro taking one card and raising.

The drummer showed his openers, two kings,
and folded.

One-Eye shook his head sadly. "You lucky
polecat," he said, and threw in his hand. "Imag-

ine drawing one card with all that money at stake."

Faro tossed his hand in the discards and drew in the pot quickly.

He was just about to stand up and call it a night when his attention was drawn to the man who was sitting opposite him. The cowboy, pretty drunk by now, had his eyes directly on One-Eye Jacobsen, but he included Faro in his view.

"You dealt seconds," he said suddenly.

One-Eye, half out of his chair, sat back down again.

"You two are working together," the cowboy said, and his hand moved just slightly; both had been on the table when he started talking, but now his right hand began to move back. "You sonsofbitches," he said.

The area immediately around the table was suddenly still. Nobody was moving. But Faro, watching that cowboy's hand creeping toward the edge of the table, suddenly moved fast. His own right hand snaked to his vest and dropped beneath the table. In the silence that lay on the scene his words were soft, but quite audible.

"I have got your crotch covered with a *pepperbox*," he said. "It's loaded and will blast your balls to smithereens. You got half a minute to git up and git out!" And as he concluded his invitation to that drunken cowboy, everyone heard an ominous click as the hammer of the gun beneath the table was drawn back.

The cowboy's hand had stopped at the table edge, and his face turned absolutely white. He started to speak, but no word came out. His mouth sagged. For a minute he looked as though he was about to burst into tears, but he didn't. Then his courage returned. He stood up. "Fuck you," he said, and turned and walked away from the table.

He had taken only a half dozen steps when suddenly he whirled, his arm striking toward his holstered six-gun.

But Marshal Cole Herkimer, walking through the batwing doors at just that point, was suddenly right up against the cowboy, pinning him in a bear hug.

"Now, you wouldn't want to mess up this nice clean saloon, would you, cowboy?" He smiled coldly, loosening his grip at the same time that his left hand drew the other's gun from its holster. "You're not allowed firearms in this town, mister. I'm being easy on you. You sober up and come back tomorrow to my office." He stepped back. "Got it?" His voice was hard as a bullet.

The cowboy nodded and without another word pushed his way through the crowd and departed.

Herkimer turned toward Faro and One-Eye Jacobsen. One-Eye was visibly shaken by the event which was evident as he stood up unsteadily and said good-night.

Herkimer looked down at Faro, who was still seated with his hands beneath the table.

"I'll take that pepperbox too, Blake," he said.

Faro brought his hands slowly from beneath the table. In his hand was a gold pocket watch, which he opened, and said, "Appears to be that time for a little liquid refreshment, eh, Marshal?" As he snapped the lid shut, all present heard the click that sounded exactly like the cocking of a pistol.

Herkimer's face broke into a big grin.
"By God, it'll be on me, Blake."

It was late when Faro left the Goldroom—late,
but not yet dawn. Honeytown lay under a deep
starry sky. Faro stood for a moment on the wide
board sidewalk, breathing in the smell of horses
and cattle. He felt good; he had that sense of
well-being which comes from a job well done.

Too late he heard the movement behind him.
The grip on his shoulder was like a vise as he
was spun, and the cigar was knocked out of his
mouth. The stench of garlic and rotten teeth left
no mistake about his attacker. The next thing
Faro knew he was flat on his back, and the side
of his head felt as if he had been hit with a
singletree. Horrible Henry McCluskie drove his
enormous boot into his victim's ribs.

"Get up, you sonofabitch," he demanded. And
reaching down grabbed Faro by the scruff of his
neck, collar and hair and dragged him up in
order to deliver further punishment. But Faro
suddenly let himself go limp in total relaxation
instead of struggling. And it served its purpose
by throwing Horrible McCluskie into surprise.

In that moment Faro drove his boot into the
other man's kneecap and then brought a sledge-
hammer blow of his fist against the doubled
McCluskie's ear. The huge man toppled.

Faro stood nearby, gasping for air; his head
felt as though he had been hit by a train, while
McCluskie dragged himself to his knees.

Before he was fully on his feet he lunged at
Faro, grabbing him around the knees and bringing him to the street. Faro pushed his thumbs
into both of Henry's eyes and pressed. The giant

released him, screaming in anguish as he did so. Faro rolled clear, pulled himself up with the aid of the saddle rig on a horse standing at the hitching rail.

Through hazy eyes he watched McCluskie charge right at him. He ducked and dove through the horse's legs. McCluskie was not quick enough to change direction and he crashed right into the horse's side. The horse, a big palomino, started to buck and kick, and suddenly Horrible Henry let out a scream of pain as one of those flying hooves caught him in the chest. Faro watched in amazement as his opponent went flying into the middle of Main Street. McCluskie lay in the street, either dead or out cold. Faro didn't care which.

The battle had brought some of the clientele out of the Goldroom, and the owner of the palomino finally appeared, but by now his horse was no longer spooked. He was still somewhat riled, standing spread-legged, his eyes rolling, and his ears moving cautiously about, while he snorted loudly. The worthies began to discuss what had happened, and while it was decided that Horrible McCluskie was not dead but had only been "cold cocked by Roy Swindell's cow pony", Faro departed quietly into the darkness of the streets.

Chapter 4

It was Faro's custom to breakfast at the Gem Eatery. He had discovered its unique cuisine on his first morning in Honeytown—arbuckle coffee, sourdough, beans—and being a man of habit he returned. The atmosphere was pleasant, meaning for him that it was in sharp contrast to those places where he plied his profession. Quiet in the morning was mandatory at certain times, and coffee was always necessary. The Gem served a good brew. Faro would dawdle over his three, four cups reviewing the action of the previous night, planning forthcoming games, checking mentally on his file on various card players and other gamesmen. Or, he often enjoyed simple conversation with whoever might be handy, or would pleasure himself sitting near the window, watching whatever was going on in the street outside.

He was doing just that, gazing out at Main Street which lay in heavy heat under a pale blue sky, when he saw the three men approaching. The trio was led by none other than Horrible Henry McCluskie. Moreover, they were approaching at a brisk and determined clip.

Something told Faro that trio was up to no good, and he unbuttoned his coat so that he could have swift and easy access to his Reid knuckle-duster/pistol. Dammit, he thought, his morning relaxation was going to be spoiled by that knothead McCluskie.

The trio burst into the Gem, to the dim surprise of the proprietor who was wiping the counter in slow strokes, not showing much vigor for the task—the day being already that warm—and to the alarm of the only other customer besides Faro. This was a small man with pale yellow hair plastered to his oblong-shaped head, an extremely red face and eyelashes so white they were all but invisible.

Blake!" McCluskie had powered himself right up to within a couple of feet of Faro while his two companions fanned out beside him, almost equally close to their quarry. "I'm challenging you to a fair fight. These here gents is going to handle it."

Faro, realizing this was no social call, kept his eyes close on McCluskie, but also allowed the other two into his awareness, seeing them more as shapes than as individuals. It was a trick he had learned years ago: never concentrate exclusively on details when confronted by more than one person—that way you could get clipped—but rather see the whole picture, loose.

McCluskie's companions were known to Faro;

he had seen them in the Goldroom. The thin one was a gambler named Bummer George Wiley; the one with the square-cut beard was a monte dealer named Jorgensen.

It was Bummer George who took over now. "Thing is, Blake, the horse race and badger fight that was goin' to be held after the preacher next Sunday is bin called off. So me an' Jorgensen here an' Henry figgered a prizefight would be a good attraction."

Jorgensen cut in. "People are all looking forward to something. They'll be listenin' to the preacher from Ellenburg and they'll be needin' something a little lively after it."

"The real reason though is I'm going to whip your hairy ass!" roared McCluskie, "and, by Jesus, you kin throw in that palomino to boot, and I'll whip him too! You fought me dirty an' I'm going to even it with the prize ring rules."

Faro looked at Horrible Henry's hands, which were the size of buffalo steaks. "Thanks," he said, "but the thing is, I don't operate in that profession. I am a gambler, and as such I have to watch my hands."

He saw that his words fell on the trio as on stone.

"We citizens of Honeytown would take it most unkind if you were to refuse our offer, Blake," said Jorgensen, and he ran his tongue around the inside of his mouth and wet his thin lips. "We have gotten the blessing of the Town Council and the marshal and everybody, I say everybody, thinks it's just a jim-dandy idee."

"Blake," roared McCluskie, "you can put yer money where yer mouth is; you can bet. You'll be on the short end, I've no doubt." And he chuckled. "By jingo, this time you won't have no goddamn stud horse fightin' for ya!"

"I don't think I'm interested," Faro said. "Though I do—"

"We think that yes would be a more suitable answer to our offer," Bummer George said, cutting in.

Faro felt something cold wash through him as he looked into those three sets of resolute eyes. "I'd like to consider it," he said. "Think it over a few days."

Bummer George swung his leg over a counter stool. "We will have us a cup of coffee," he said, "during which time you can decide whether you want to fight bareknuckle or with gloves."

"Gloves?"

"These." Jorgensen took a pair of skin-tight riding gloves out of his coat pocket.

Faro had seen fights with such gloves. They were more damaging than bare knuckles, for the ridges along the knuckles were able to cut like knives. They could literally carve an opponent to pieces. He had fought bareknuckled a few times, but never with gloves, though he had seen one or two glove fights. He clearly remembered the battle out in Bakersfield a few years back. It lasted 120 rounds London Prize Ring rules with both fighters cut to ribbons about the face. Faro for sure had no wish to travel 120 rounds, or even 20 with the likes of Horrible Henry McCluskie. But he could also see he was in no place to argue the issue.

Now, his smile wry, he said, "Well, since you put your offer in that way, I don't rightly feel I can refuse." And he sat down next to Jorgensen. "Like you say, I am a gambling man. And so, I shall take this opportunity to turn a few earnest, if hard-earned, dollars by meeting this big lummox and I will whip the living shit out of his blubbery carcass." And he stood up and walked swiftly out of the lunch room, leaving the trio gasping in surprise. Faro was almost laughing now as he walked down Main Street. Having decided he would go ahead with it, he had also decided he would start his psychological warfare right now. By God, he was going to need all the advantage he could get.

Faro had not engaged in an extended battle of fisticuffs, that is, a prizefight, for some while. He was good at fighting: fast, with remarkable reflexes, tough and shrewd in his strategy and remorseless under the exigencies of battle. He was also always close to top condition.

Horrible Henry, on the other hand, was a grizzly bear, a mad buffalo, a crazed longhorn high on loco weed; in short, a destroyer. Faro had no illusions about the fight being fair.

When Faro returned to the Chicago House, the desk clerk handed him a note. It was from Evelyn Sutcliff, inviting him to a dinner party at her home with some friends. The handwriting was clear, and the message precise. Since he was a substantial depositor in her bank, she thought it would be nice if he could meet some of the other important people in town with whom the bank did business.

To say that Faro Blake had ever overlooked the salient points of an attractive woman would have been a fantastic understatement, in short a lie; and yet, that evening, when he encountered Evelyn Sutcliff for the second time in his life he would have had to be the first to admit to such an accusation. For indeed, his hostess, greeting him with a charm and sensuality that threw him very nearly into confusion, drove the thought of anyone else right out of his mind. Faro was used to women approaching him from their animal appetite, but Evelyn Sutcliff was clearly not the usual female. She was obviously quite something else.

At the bank, only two days before, she had been attractive, yes, but a banker and widow of a banker—intelligent, lively, but not at all what he would have expected in the form of this delightful creature holding his hand in greeting and smiling teasingly up into his eyes as if she already knew carnally all about him.

The young woman who stood on the threshold of her home, his hostess, was so excitingly lovely—with her creamy skin, her cobalt blue eyes, which seemed to Faro flecked with gold— that his heart pounded as it had not done in years.

"How good of you to come, Mister Blake." Her voice matched her sensuous looks; it had the soft measure of velvet, the insistent resonance of nascent sexuality. Faro felt everything inside him melting.

They stood together in the tastefully decorated and spotlessly clean hallway. He could feel her like a magnet, and as she led him into the large living room he had to force himself into a neutral attitude.

"I do so want you to meet some of Honeytown's important people, Mister Blake."

It was an attractively furnished room, with a number of people standing and sitting, engaged in lively conversation. There were some dozen men and women: cattle buyers from the East, government men buying for the Indian reservations, local businessmen and ranchers. Cole Herkimer was there, and one other man whom he recognized as a face only, a member of the audience when he had played with One-Eye Jacobsen.

Following introductions, Faro found himself watching his hostess—it was nigh impossible to not look at her—and at the same time listening to a story Cole Herkimer was relating in his deep, plangent voice.

"You don't believe it?" the marshal was saying as a burst of laughter greeted his tale. "Harry Bronson was an extraordinary man. Educated at Harvard college, a teacher by profession until he became an outlaw; the only thing, as I've told you, is he simply could not sit a horse."

"Incredible."

"It's a grand tale."

"And it is true," Herkimer insisted. "He is known as the outlaw who couldn't ride. He'd pull off some really daring jobs on banks and trains and stages, but he invariably got caught."

"Because his horse threw him!"

"Right."

"What happened to Bronson finally?"

"He's in Folsom prison for life."

Evelyn, sweeping across the room, trilled with laughter. "You must have a bag full of exciting stories, Marshal Herkimer. And you too, Mister Blake. I understand you have traveled a good deal."

"I have been around," Faro said, smiling. "My profession often requires traveling."

The man who had witnessed Faro's game at

the Goldroom said, "Marshal Herkimer, I have heard that you used to be up around Alder Gulch in Montana."

Faro thought he saw a shadow pass across Herkimer's face, but it was so fleeting he told himself he must be mistaken.

"I did spend some time around Virginia City," Herkimer replied easily.

"Then more than likely you were there when Henry Plummer was about."

"Ah, yes. Sheriff Plummer made quite a mark on the community there," said Herkimer.

The man who had asked about Henry Plummer said, "I understand he was nobody to mess with." The speaker was bald, and he ran the palm of his hand quickly across his head as he finished speaking, as though wiping rather than feeling it. And Faro remembered that Evelyn had introduced him as Patrick Tebeau, a cattle dealer from Denver.

"But who is this Plummer person?" asked a young lady in a black satin dress, the wife of a wealthy eastern cattle buyer. "Why are we talking about him?"

Patrick Tebeau answered her immediately. "Because he was what the newspapers call 'colorful.' He was a murderer, supposed to have been responsible for over a hundred killings around Virginia City and Alder Gulch in a single year. I know Granny Stuart who organized the vigilantes to get him."

"But somebody said he was the sheriff. . . ." insisted the lady in black.

"He was. He was the sheriff and at the same time he was running the outlaws—robbing and killing, and of course never getting caught."

"He was also a gambler," put in Herkimer. "And a highly cultured man. He'd been to college apparently, read books. All that."

"Nobody ever knew where he came from," Tebeau said. "He was a man of mystery."

"But they sure knew where he went," Faro said.

"To hell apparently," someone said, and the company enjoyed a laugh at that sleek observation.

"Oh, let's not talk of such morbid matters," Evelyn said. "Besides, everybody ought to be good and hungry by now."

It was just at this point that a new arrival appeared, offering no apology for lateness, Faro noted. He was introduced as Hobart Maxwell. A flamboyant Texas rancher, Maxwell had ridden into town ahead of his trail herd, which was still a couple of days south of Honeytown.

A stocky man in his forties, Maxwell had small eyes close together and a loud voice and brash manner. Yet he was at home in the company, though tending always to dominate the conversation. It turned out that he had met Evelyn through the bank on his last trip north.

The gathering settled down to dinner, and by now Faro had figured out the various characters. The lady seated on his left, wife of a government man on Indian business who sat across from her, turned in her seat and said, "It must be exciting to be a gambler, Mister Blake. You said you do a good bit of traveling."

Faro caught Herkimer's eye at that and could hardly suppress a smile.

"It is true, ma'am."

Evelyn cut in. "But why are there no lady

gamblers, Mister Blake? You know, I have always wanted to learn to gamble."

"But there are," said Tebeau.

The government man said, "There have been some famous ones."

"What about Poker Alice, for example?" Patrick Tebeau said. "She's famous enough I'd say." And he laughed.

"Poker Alice? What a marvelous name."

"Where does she, uh, ply her trade?" Evelyn asked, her eyes on Faro.

Faro responded quickly. "She's all over—mostly Colorado, Denver and Creede, but Alice gets about."

"Have you ever encountered this fascinating lady, Mister Blake?"

Faro laughed. "I certainly have. I have admired her over the years, and I have always favored her brand of cigars." This brought a big round of laughter from the dinner table.

Faro remembered clearly Alice Duffield with her big cigar, and he also remembered the .45 she pulled on a crooked dealer that time in Creede.

"California's the place for women and gambling," Maxwell cut in, looking over at Faro. "I presume you've been there, Blake." His tone, the expression on his round face, everything about the man was filled with arrogance. Faro found him extremely distasteful. But his voice was even when he spoke.

"Yes, I've been there." He smiled to cover his dislike of the Texan, but his blood still rose at the look on Maxwell's face.

It was the only moment in the evening when there was any note of dissension. He wondered why Maxwell had tried to needle him, but put it down to the man's nature as a bully.

The dinner, Faro noted, was superb. He decided that Evelyn Sutcliff knew how to do things well. And he couldn't help but compare her to Janey Hand. The contrast couldn't have been greater; and yet, he found himself drawn to both. Ruefully, he wondered what it was in himself that appreciated and even needed such contrasts. It was, in fact, something he liked about himself.

"You serve an impressive dinner, Mrs. Sutcliff," he heard himself saying. There was a murmur of instant agreement from the company. "I've had nothing like this since I last dined in San Francisco at Winn's Fountain Head."

"Ah, you known Winn's," said a tall man with a thick mustache and eyebrows—a cattle dealer. "I love Winn's. They serve the best oysters, and the venison . . ." He paused in midair, as it were, and added quickly, "is almost as good as Mrs. Sutcliff's." His recovery was perfect, and everyone laughed appreciably at the way he had handled it.

Glaring at Faro, Maxwell returned to the charge. "You like California, huh?" It sounded almost like an accusation the way it was put.

Faro looked slowly at the Texan. Stocky, as though padded with money, he reflected, but held together with a rage for the world. "I like gold," Faro said, and his tone was bland. His remark, so flatly put, brought a volley of laughter.

Faro was indeed at his charming best, all southern, all Kentucky bourbon and horses, flashing teeth and eyes, sandy hair and high cheekbones giving him the look of a cougar on the prowl—really a true dandy. He knew th' with the exception of Maxwell, he had wo company.

"I have heard that everyone in San Francisco is a millionaire," the lady in the black satin gown said. "They say the miners all have gold-nugget watch chains."

A short man with puffy cheeks, in which were revealed a lot of blue veins, said, "The streets are paved with money." Someone had told Faro that he was the owner of Honeywell's General Store.

"Do you know the difference between a San Francisco millionaire and a Chicago million-aire?" Faro asked, and he saw Maxwell glower-ing at the attention he was receiving.

The owner of Honeywell's General Store spread his hands with his palms up and smiled.

"What *is* the difference?" Evelyn asked.

"When a San Franciscan makes a million he builds a stable with marble halls, Brussels carpet and hot and cold water in every stall."

"And what does a Chicago millionaire do?"

"He builds a college."

Faro's timing was skillful; he was an ace raconteur, and the company loved it.

But Hobart Maxwell had been left out of it for too long, and he now launched himself onto center stage.

"Far as I am concerned, them San Francis-cans with all their gold cannot ever beat out a poke full of genuine diamonds."

"Diamonds, you say?"

"Diamonds I say." Maxwell sniffed. He even managed what Faro thought was a smile. "You all have heard of the diamonds found in Africa last year. And there has been another strike, even bigger diamonds and just a few miles away from the first."

"That's fine for Africa," someone said. "Be good if we could find some diamonds right here in Kansas."

"It's been good for me," Maxwell said. And suddenly everyone's attention was on him. "I don't mind telling you, I have been down south of the border in Old Mexico about a month back, and I got me a bag full of the genuine article."

"Diamonds?"

"Big as a horse's tooth, every durn one of 'em." Maxwell chuckled. It sounded to Faro like a crow cawing in a cornfield. "What with the revolution going on down there, you can pick up stuff. Though," he quickly added, "it wasn't all luck. It was smart, too, by God."

"You should put that kind of thing in the bank," Evelyn said. "Not that I am looking for business. But you could get robbed."

And all at once Maxwell reached beneath his coat and brought out a leather sack. He chuckled as the company leaned forward in a brisk spur of interest.

"Diamonds," he said softly, opening the sack and spilling its contents onto the table.

There was a measured silence as everyone looked at the gems. Then, Maxwell swept them into the leather bag. He had indeed gained their full attention, Faro noted.

Maxwell snapped out a laugh. "I can handle myself. Besides, I like to have that much valuables right next to my skin." He coughed out another laugh. "Don't get the idea that a man can reach sizable wealth—I say sizable— without running somethin' other than hairy old longhorns." And his little eyes completely disappeared in his thick face as he fell into gasping, almost silent, laughing.

He had evidently had much to drink, and Faro now saw that Herkimer was watching Maxwell closely. The Texan could be troublesome under the influence, no doubt about that. Still, he did keep within bounds, simply bragging about his diamonds.

"I tell you, I have been not only a rancher, but I fought the bandits, and I bin a rootin-tootin freebooter. I am taking my poke of diamonds, heading back East and finding me a cute little filly an' hitch myself right to her."

Faro watched Evelyn, for Maxwell was just bordering on impropriety; but their hostess listened calmly, as though Maxwell had been discussing the weather or some other innocuous matter.

It was now that Herkimer put in a word. "I should warn you, Maxwell, not to talk about this outside this room. We've been having some robberies around Honeytown lately, and I think it's an organized gang. If anyone got wind of what you are carrying on your person, then you could find yourself in trouble."

"Marshal, I can handle myself. Don't worry about it." And Maxwell laughed.

"I would listen to the Marshal, if I were you, Maxwell," Tebeau said. "You are more than safe here with a lawman like Cole Herkimer, but you can't be too careful. I imagine those diamonds of yours are worth a whole lot."

"I can handle it, never fear," Maxwell said sourly. "I'll be heading back to my herd tomorrow in any case," he added, looking over at Evelyn Sutcliff, as though suddenly realizing he had been boorish.

"Marshal, has anything happened on the robberies? Have you turned up any clues?" It was a short woman with heavy arms and a lot of jewelry who asked the question.

"Afraid not anything to speak of, ma'am," Herkimer replied. "But we are working on it."

It was ten o'clock when the evening drew to a close. One by one the guests took their departure from the gracious hostess. Faro was among the last to leave. Shaking hands with Evelyn Sutcliff, he was surprised to find a piece of paper slipped into his palm. As soon as he was alone he read the message. "Midnight. Back door. Two knocks."

Walking back to his hotel with Cole Herkimer, Faro pondered the note, surprised that she had been that forward. Of course, the note might not necessarily be sexual in demand; maybe the lady was in trouble and wanted a helping hand, a listening ear, advice. Well, he told himself, in a couple of hours he would find out.

They were approaching the Chicago House through an alley when a figure suddenly emerged, came up to Herkimer and began talking in a whisper.

As they walked toward the hotel, Herkimer said, "That was Farkas from over at Tenant Wells. He thinks he has a lead on the gang we were talking about this evening. I'll be riding over there tonight."

And with a nod he was gone.

Faro found no time to concern himself with bandits or Tenant Wells. His whole concern was with the sort of reception he would be given when he knocked twice on Mrs. Sutcliff's back door at midnight. Looking at the clock on the wall, he saw that he still had a whole hour to go.

Chapter 5

If Faro was concerned over the sort of reception he would run into at midnight at Evelyn Sutcliff's, he was soon put at ease.

She was wearing a silk gown which literally clung to her superb figure, and he could hardly keep his hands off her as she led the way into the parlor.

Turning, she smiled at him. "Mister Blake, I must apologize for calling you out at this late hour, but . . . well, I suppose it is silly. I can be silly, you know. But . . . well, during the day it seems I never have time to do the things I want, what with the bank and all that. . . ." She paused, pouring brandy for each of them and handing him his glass. "Well, I wanted you to teach me how to play poker." She laughed suddenly, just a bit embarrassed, and he liked that. "There it is. I'm just dying to learn."

"I'll show you anything you want, Mrs. Sutcliff—as long as I am able that is."

"Won't you please call me Evelyn?"

"If you'll do me the same."

"Faro."

"What sort of poker, Evelyn?"

"I don't know. What sort do you have?" She laughed. "Actually, I'm not completely ignorant; I used to play a little with my husband."

"Have you a deck of cards?"

"Oh, yes."

He had his own, which he always carried, but he felt somehow that he wanted to see hers. It was a brand new pack she brought forth.

"I'll show you straight draw poker for a start," he said, and then, smiling, "only because you put out such a great dinner."

She laughed. He soon discovered she was a quick learner, and he liked that. He liked smart women.

"See," he told her. "You have to study people. That's the whole thing if you want to win at cards. Study your own weaknesses as well as those of your opponents." As they ran through a few hands he illustrated what his points were and kept up a commentary on what he was doing, what the possibilities were, the dangers, the various strategies.

"Always keep a poker face. Keep silent. Don't complain when you lose a hand or gloat when you win. Never drink while playing. If you watch yourself, your opponents and the game itself, you'll have plenty to think about. Drinking leads to carelessness, and it's just too easy to tip your hand."

"It's a lot to remember," Evelyn said.

"It's a lot to forget," he told her. "So know that it's better to remember it than to forget it." He paused and then went on. "You say you've watched games. Notice how the winners all chatter, and the losers remain silent."

"That is right!" She was obviously very pleased at the way he was teaching her.

He found himself telling her about the game he had played with One-Eye Jacobsen and the drummer and the drunken cowboy.

"But you see, One-Eye intentionally chose to play straight draw instead of deuces wild."

"Why did he do that?"

Faro smiled at her eagerness. "See, except for me—and One-Eye wasn't sure about me—the other players were mostly inexperienced. For instance, in deuces wild if you stand pat, they will think you have a straight, flush or a full house, any one of which can be beat easily. If you draw one in deuces, though, they know the four deuces and the joker are wild, and they're dumb enough to figure you're drawing to a straight, flush or two pair. Now, in draw, I can stand pat any time I want to, and the player has to figure for himself whether I'm bluffing or not. Look, suppose you open the pot, and I raise and stand pat. Will you call me if you don't fill your hand, which prohibitive odds say you won't?"

"But you say that One-Eye kept making that play over and over."

"Sure. But you see, he set up the drummer for just that play, wanting him to think he was bluffing."

"But he might have filled his hand."

"Sure, he *might* have. A lot of people know that play, and probably a lot of people spot how often One-Eye uses it. It's like odd and even. First you have them, then you don't. Keep them guessing is the point. And when you think you have them beat, play your hand hard. It's the law of averages that wins poker for you. That's the rule: set up your man with a bluff, then knock him down with the winning hand."

While he was speaking she kept her eyes right on him, watching his every gesture, catching every word.

"Aren't you afraid of giving away your professional secrets?" she asked him as she replenished their glasses.

Faro shook his head. "There are no secrets. It's all in the play. If you're sharp to the play, that's the point. Otherwise, you can have a barrel of secrets and it won't do you an inch of good." He chuckled suddenly. "My dad used to tell me that the best secret is one that everybody knows already, but nobody can do."

She looked puzzled. "How do you mean that?"

"I'll tell you what he said when I asked him that same question. He said, 'It's exactly like being honest. Everybody knows it, and nobody can do it. It's a public secret; you'll never have to worry about anyone being able to reveal it.'"

Evelyn Sutcliff threw back her head and laughed, setting the top front of her gown to rippling in a way that impressed Faro mightily. He had been pretty sure that she wasn't whaleboned up under the gown, but the laugh made the matter clear. She said, "That's true of so many things, isn't it? There are things you know, but you can't reveal them—and awfully few people can do them, at least do them right?"

"What kinds of things, ma'am?" Faro said,

leaning back, amused. Funny how some women seemed to have to make a whole vaudeville act out of this stuff—the polite conversation, the poker instruction and so on, all leading up to where they just about were now. Mrs. S. was horny and had roped him out of the herd for the job, and there it was. But she wasn't content to let it go at that; there had to be this big dance around beforehand.

"Things it doesn't do to *talk* about," she said with mock primness. She crossed her legs with a soft whispering sound that might have been the rustle of the gown or the sliding of one silk-stockinged thigh over the other.

"Be a thought to conduct a discussion of such topics in sign language, like the Indians use," Faro said. "Nobody'd have to use shaming verbiage, but the point'd get across, if you'll excuse the expression."

She was signing pretty well herself by now, he thought. The smooth drape of the silk over her breasts was interrupted by two neatly centered bumps that had swelled up visibly in the last minute. There was a breathy quality to her voice, and she was once again recrossing her legs.

She refilled their brandy glasses, leaning closer to him, bringing him the scent of her perfume and a sharper musky odor. "What sort of signs would you use?"

"Well, for basics, there's one goes 'way back, thousands of years; they call it 'the fig.'" He made a fist of his right hand and thrust the thumb between the first and second fingers.

Evelyn Sutcliff took his wrist and drew the clenched hand close to her, studying it. "What's

that supposed to stand for . . . ? Oh . . . Mr.
Blake, that's not really very *proper!*" She firmly
opened the offending fist and encircled the base
of the thumb with her fingers, squeezing it.
"There, I've changed your sign for one of my
own."

And a damned effective one; Faro felt his
erection straining at his trousers with a sudden
lurch that threatened the stability of his fly
buttons. Evelyn Sutcliff released his hand, and
there seemed hardly anything to do with it but
let it drop two inches to the thin silk that lay over
her breasts. He circled a stiff nipple with his
forefinger and thumb, then pressed it. "Now,
that's a sign that comes from pushing a door-
bell, ma'am. Means the same thing, see—
requesting permission to enter."

Her mouth was slack and her eyes half-closed.
"What . . . what's the sign for 'Please come in'?"
Her hands were wandering over his vest, then
downward across the belly of his trousers, strok-
ing.

"I think you just came across it," Faro said
hoarsely. His hands slid around to the back of
the gown, and his fingers began working busily
at its fastenings. He recalled fleetingly that first
time, back when he was thirteen, and a touch,
when Mrs. Ducharme had enlivened her upriver
journey by instructing him in just what went on
between a man and a woman. He had fumbled
haplessly at the row of tiny buttons that held her
dress together until their joint urgencies had
obliged them to finish the job by sliding off her
drawers and working upward through her volu-
minous skirts. Afterward, she had made him

unfasten and refasten the buttons until he gained dexterity, and the skill had stayed with him through the years since. In a few seconds the silk whispered away from Evelyn Sutcliff's shoulders and arms, and his face was buried between her breasts, slick with sweat, yet cool.

She moaned and clutched at his still-trousered erection with frank hunger. He pushed her hand aside and began to thumb open his trouser buttons.

To Faro's stupefaction, she stiffened and drew away. "Not here," she said faintly. "Upstairs . . . my room."

"It's just as good on the sofa, or the rug if it comes to that," Faro said urgently. This was the damn *moment*, and he didn't cotton to the notion of climbing a flight of stairs while bent double by his constricted pecker, or else with his trousers unbuttoned and the damn thing wagging in the night air.

"No!" She twisted away from him and headed for the parlor door, her bared back gleaming above the tumble of silk at her waist.

He followed, hobbling and hissing curses under his breath, out into the hall and up the staircase. As she turned at the top of the stairs, an oil lamp hung on the wall cast warm light on her breasts—which were bobbing with her swift walk—and his irritation was forgotten, burned away in a new surge of lust.

He did not take in the details of the bedroom, except for the large bed, topped by a deep purple comforter. Evelyn Sutcliff stood facing him in front of it, naked to the waist, her creamy skin, lightly filmed with moisture, glowing in the

light of the single lamp. Her dress was in a
puddle of fabric at her feet, and she was clad
only in embroidered linen drawers and open-
work stockings. Her breasts were not girlishly
high and firm, but ample and still short of
sagging; the erect nipples, surrounded by wide
circles of pale rose, pointed slightly down and
outward. Mrs. S. is one of your ripely mature
kind, Faro decided. He had never been able to
figure whether it was better with this sort of
woman or the younger, lither ones, but it had
been a hell of a lot of fun exploring the proposi-
tion.

"You want to hang your dress up?" Faro asked.
"Get wrinkled, lying there that way." Once he
had been deep in the throes of passion with a
woman who had, close to the crisis, suddenly
been smitten with concern about her ball gown
and insisted on arranging it so as to guard
against creases. He had carried on his end of
things afterward capably enough, but the enthu-
siasm had dimmed. It was now his practice to
make sure in advance that that kind of detail
would not come up.

Evelyn Sutcliff cast a glance at the door of the
bedroom closet, which stood slightly ajar. "*Fuck
the wrinkles*," she said, and kicked the dress to
one side. Faro laughed, caught her by the hips
and flung her backward onto the bed. He peeled
her drawers away, then the stockings, and flung
them to join the rumpled gown on the floor; the
musky odor of her body intensified as it was fully
bared. Their hands collided as they joined in
stripping his clothes from his stocky frame.

He knelt, poised above her, knees sinking into
the comforter and the soft mattress beneath.

"Oh, my!" she said. "You're so big—you could hurt me."

Faro blinked. He was well endowed, he knew—certainly, there had never been any complaints on that score—but he was also nothing that you'd want to exhibit as a prodigy of nature. Maybe she was one of those finicky women, or maybe it was her way of flattering him. "Never knew one of these"—he guided her hand to enclose him—"was too much for one of *these*." He probed her with his fingers, sliding into her warmth and moisture.

"Oh . . . that's wonderful, your hand there. Now, yes, yes, come into me . . . oh, now you're in me . . . oh, I don't *believe* it, so far in, so big . . . oh, more, Christ, there *is* more, oh . . ."

Faro, moving slowly, learning her constrictions and gentle spasms, felt, mingling with the drive of his lust, a flicker of irritation. *She* knows what we're doing, he thought, and where everything's at at the moment, and, sure to God, so do *I*—we don't need no carnival barker's spiel about it.

Her thighs were locked about him, her ample breasts moving in astonishing arabesques, as their frenzy mounted. "Oh, it's like nothing I ever . . . oh, I'm coming, I . . ."

Faro drove on with drumbeat swiftness and brought himself to his climax as she achieved hers.

"Oh, that was marvelous. It was as though you'd exploded in me like a rocket. And now it's so nice, you on top of me, like a lovely living quilt, and still in me . . . so nice."

Faro lay atop her, breathing heavily. It was pleasing to have the testimonial, but it was surely something out of the way to have a sort of running appraisal made of the whole proceedings.

"Oh, you're getting smaller; I can feel it."

"'S what usually happens," Faro said.

"I bet I know a way to make you big again. If I took you in my mouth and then . . ."

For a banker, Mrs. Sutcliff had some original ideas, Faro allowed. Within five minutes they were joined again, this time in a complex position she said she had always wanted to try, and which she described in detail.

"Oh, I've come twice this time, I feel like I'm melting away . . . oh, magnificent, you're still hard, oh . . ."

When they finally concluded this second passage, Faro was aware that he had exhausted his resources for the occasion and pulled his clothes on, expressing his profound appreciation and firm farewell. To his surprise, Evelyn Sutcliff accompanied him downstairs, still naked, and kissed him at the doorway. "I don't get many depositors like you, Mr. Blake," she said. "You'll see that I have to make the most of them."

Walking back to the Chicago House in the pre-dawn, Faro reflected that this had been a unique experience. About as intense sexually as anything he'd had, and with that weird overlay of constant talk. Did Evelyn, he wondered, not really believe she was fucking unless she was describing the act in each particular?

It had been a good night's fun, no mistake— but why did he feel as if he'd somehow been *used*?

Chapter 6

Sunday dawned in total clarity. Not a cloud could be seen. By noon, heat had drugged the town and the drinking establishments were jammed with thirsty, sweating customers. There was much betting, with the odds heavily on Horrible Henry.

Faro had insisted on having a say in the selection of referee, pushing hard for Cole Herkimer. But the McCluskie contingent had objected strenuously, and they had reason, as Faro had to agree. The final choice fell to to an individual known as Cupid Towne.

Mister Towne had been born with the name Algernon. How he had ever gained the sobriquet "Cupid" was a mystery which no one had ever had the courage or stupidity to probe. For Cupid Towne was, as someone put it, "no kid with a bow and arrow and short pants." He was tough, ornery and mean as a coyote. Once, it had been reported to Faro, Cupid had killed a man for asking him why he was wearing such a bright shirt. The unfortunate victim had no way of knowing before he asked his question that Cupid was just damn fed up with people asking him about his bright red shirt, which had been given him by his lady friend, who had immediately taken off with another man, and that he had one hell of a hangover to boot. In any event, Cupid was the third man in the ring that bright afternoon in Honeytown, Kansas, when Faro Blake and Horrible Henry McCluskie were introduced as the participants in "The Fight of the Century."

Just about the entire town was present at the festivities, which was billed as a fight to the finish for the "Championship of Honeytown, Kansas."

In his corner Faro had the able assistance of Homer Tyng, and the Goldroom's number-one bartender Cyrus Mohuskie. It was the job of Tyng and Mohuskie to see that Horrible Henry's handlers didn't slip any foreign agents into his gloves, and that the referee saw to it that the fight was at least reasonably fair.

As McCluskie stepped into the ring and disrobed, the odds on him soared. He was truly a giant—six foot four and 225 pounds. Faro also drew a cheer from the crowd as he stripped for action, for his body was beautifully proportioned. He just tipped six feet in height and weighed in at 180. Thus, the difference in avoirdupois was 45 pounds, and there was also a large difference in reach. But Faro's body was as solid and compact as cord wood, with the muscles rippling like snakes under his smooth skin. He moved to his corner with the grace of a mountain lion. He had let his beard grow so that there was a two-day stubble which he would use to massage McCluskie's neck and face when the fighting was in close. Horrible, on the other hand, still carried his full growth of whiskers.

Looking down at the crowd at ringside, Faro spotted Janey Hand and some of the clientele from the Goldroom, but he didn't wish to look further for the simple reason that he wanted no distractions. The ring was pitched on turf down by the stockyards. People crowded around it; many others had climbed onto the roof of the nearby depot, and some were standing on top of a boxcar on a siding.

Both fighters had bet heavily on themselves, Cupid Towne holding the stakes. Cupid was a square-shaped man, hard as iron, with black hair close to his head and a trim mustache. He was in shirtsleeves with garters on the arms. A red bandanna handkerchief could be seen sticking out of his hip pocket. Now he motioned the fighters and their handlers to the center of the ring while the murmur of the crowd rose to a roar.

"There will be no butting, biting, hair pulling, kicking or gouging," he said, his voice hard. "A round ends when the man is down, and he better make it to scratch or I count him out. Them's London Prize Ring rules. Let me see your shoes; no spikes. And let me see those gloves." He examined these articles carefully. "Any fouling, I give the fight to the other man. Remember one thing: what I say goes. Now git to your corner and come out fightin'."

The fighters returned to their corners while the crowd roared. McCluskie was wearing long tights with an American flag around his waist as a belt. He had gotten the idea of the flag from watching heavyweight champion John C. Heenan, "The Benicia Boy," a few years back. Faro, lacking tights, wore his oldest trousers, tied with cord at the ankles.

The ring that had been put up consisted of stakes, one at each of the four corners, and two strands of rope. The crowd kept pressing in so that the referee had to keep ordering them back. In this he was assisted by Cole Herkimer and two of the Town Council.

It was clear to all that Faro's advantage would only be in speed, for McCluskie had it over him in everything else—height, weight, reach and brute strength.

"Don't let him close with you," Tyng had warned over and over. It was advice that wasn't necessary, for Faro had no notion at all of allowing the giant that advantage. He knew that if he ever let McCluskie get his arms around him he would be crushed.

But there was one other advantage that Faro held, and which was to become evident in a short while. This was the matter of physical condition.

At a signal from Cupid Towne the hostler at Dunn's livery whose name was Harold—no one knew if he had any other name—hit the side of the bell with a silver dollar several times. And the fight was on.

Faro moved slowly out of his corner while McCluskie charged across the ring. The big man began throwing punches all over the place, trying at the same time to close with his smaller opponent. Faro received a tremendous right to the chest, and another to his right bicep. The blow felt as though it had broken his arm. The next thing he knew, McCluskie had closed and had his arms tight around him in a bearhug. In a trice he had backheeled Faro to the ground, landing with all his 225 pounds right on top of him. Thus ended round one.

Faro made it all right to scratch and retaliated now by coming in with a hard butt under the giant's whiskers, followed by a right and then a left-hand smash into Henry's solar plexus and a right to the kidney. McCluskie staggered and the crowd roared. Faro drove in and then in a flash he was wrapped in another bearhug; but this time he ran his beard stubble like coarse sandpaper over his opponent's eyes until Mc-Cluskie's grip slackened. Meanwhile, Faro tromped as hard as he could on the other man's instep.

But again Faro was brought to the ground, this time by a crashing blow to the shoulder. It didn't seem to matter where Horrible Henry hit him, the blow was lethal. Between rounds Homer Tyng and Cyrus Mohuskie sloshed water on him, fanned him with a towel and offered the brandy bottle. But Faro was not in the mood for strong liquid.

In the next round he circled McCluskie, trying to draw him off balance. In a flash, Horrible was at him, raking him across the eyes with the stitching on his gloves, and in close, bringing his knee into Faro's crotch. As the sickening wave of pain hit Faro, Cupid Towne was pulling them apart, swearing at McCluskie, threatening to knock the shit out of the big man personally if he didn't fight fair.

The sun was dazzling, and both fighters were streaming with sweat and blood, too, from a cut over Faro's eye and a long slash on McCluskie's jaw.

The brutal heat of the sun drove into their surging bodies. Now Faro brought his knee into McCluskie's kneecap, and with a gasping curse, Horrible fell back a step, though still on his feet, while Faro bore in, swinging short hooks and choppers followed now and again by a long overhand right to the head. Now he landed a left uppercut into the liver, another into the solar plexus and a tremendous overhand, looping right to the jaw. The big man suddenly crashed down onto his seat with his legs and arms outspread, a look of utter surprise on his face.

The crowd screamed their delight at the turn the battle had momentarily taken as betting briskly fluctuated, and Faro began to be more favored. The fighters clinched, both men using elbows to advantage, while the infighting was even more vicious, Horrible Henry shoving his thumb into Faro's eye, butting him on the bridge of his nose and stepping hard on his feet.

In round twenty-two the pace quickened, to everyone's surprise. Until now McCluskie had shown the advantage, although Faro was definitely in the running. At the start of the round Henry smashed a right into Faro's face, and a left to the body drove him halfway across the ring, Faro trying to cover as McCluskie followed close. The crowd went berserk as, with a powerful chopping right, McCluskie drove his smaller opponent into the ropes. Then the giant was on top of him, Faro hanging halfway out of the ring while McCluskie, his face contorted in rage, tried to twist the ring rope around Faro's neck. It took Cupid Towne, Cole Herkimer and three others to get McCluskie off him.

At this point the referee wanted to award the fight to Faro on a foul, but Faro would have none of it. He was furious now, and his rage brought fresh force to his body.

In the twenty-third round Faro slipped from his corner, his battle plan clear now. McCluskie powered across the ring, landing a left swing on Faro's arm and then, planting himself in the center of the ring, he began punching as Faro moved swiftly around him, always moving to McCluskie's left, stabbing with his left jab at his opponent's eyes. For by now the giant's left eye was completely closed, and he could see only out of his right. Now Faro smashed at McCluskie's good eye in an effort to close it as well. And he butted him in the clinch for good measure. Neither battler heard Cupid Towne's warnings over fouling any longer.

The crowd was shrieking for the kill as McCluskie, blinded now, staggered about the ring, with Faro bobbing and weaving, dancing in and out and landing his punches almost at will, until at last, he brought his huge opponent down flat on his back with a tremendous right into which Faro put everything he had.

At the start of the twenty-fourth round, Faro returned to McCluskie's eyes. The giant could hardly see Faro as a blur, let alone see his shape or where he was coming from. The crowd was chanting now for Faro to finish it. It was at this moment that McCluskie reached over the ropes as one of his seconds handed him the stool on which he sat between rounds. In a flash he had thrown it right at Faro; but to the delight of the crowd, Faro ducked in time.

Now Faro forged in, ducking, bobbing and weaving out of reach of the helpless giant. In close, he shifted his stance and brought a powerful uppercut to the solar plexus, another to the heart and a chopping right under McCluskie's ear as he started down. Horrible Henry fell as though he had been poleaxed. Nobody expected him to get up. The "Fight of the Century" was over. And Faro, staggering across the ring was all but mobbed by the shrieking crowd, while referee Cupid Towne held his arm aloft in victory.

Faro was physically aware of the battering he had taken, but exultation flooded through him in a warming, invigorating tide. He felt able to take on five more Horrible Henrys, wrangle a Brahma bull to the ground, eat ten steak dinners, drink his way through a case of bourbon, or hump his way through a regiment of women. He felt foolishly happy and powerful—and suspected dimly that his wits had gotten a little sprung from the fight, though that didn't seem important at the moment.

He pushed away from the throng of well-wishers and winning bettors who pressed around to congratulate him, and followed a trim figure he saw walking ahead of him as the crowd dispersed.

"Some fight, Mr. Blake," Janey Hand said as he caught up with her.

"You got to get back to the Goldroom right now, Janey Hand?" Faro asked thickly.

"No, I'm off 'til seven. Fight pretty much killed the noon trade, so's it wasn't worthwhile to open. Why you askin'?"

"I want to fuck you, Janey Hand, thass why." Faro was aware that the statement could have been put more gracefully, but could not at the moment dredge up the polite form of words.

"Mr. Blake!" Janey glared at him. "I'm no whore, even if I do come from Hide Park!"

"No whoring into it," Faro said. "Wasn't thinking of *paying*, Janey Hand. See, Janey Hand, I just beat the shit out of the town bully, just won the Fight of the Century, just cleaned up one hell of a lot in side bets I had the sand to place on myself. Well, just so the day won't be a total loss, I figure I got to get to bed with the prettiest woman around here, Janey Hand. And don't tell me thass not you."

"You got a way with a compliment, for sure," Janey Hand said, looking at him intently. "My belief, you're what they call punchdrunk, Mr. Blake, so I won't take offense. But I don't think you're safe in the streets in your condition so I'll see you to your room and get you settled so's you can rest up."

Faro's ebullient mood weakened a little as he experienced unexpected difficulty in navigating the stairs at the Chicago House, and he was glad to flop heavily onto the bed.

Janey Hand slid him out of his jacket and undid his shirt. "That's quite a collection of bruises you got, Mr. Blake. You're going to be some stiff for a while."

"Should see the other guy, Janey Hand," Faro said.

"I did. I was there, remember?"

"Oh, yeah."

She went to the washstand, dipped a rag in the water pitcher and returned to sponge off the sweat and dried blood from his scrapes. "Hurt much anywheres else?"

He patted a thigh. "Sumbitch kicked me. Like a damn horse. Horsible Henry, ha?"

"Oh, hell," she said. "Way you are, it can't do any harm." With practiced deftness, she undid his trousers and pulled them down and off. "These is now your third best, even if you only got two pair, she said, holding them up. "The dust, blood and such'll come out in the wash, but there's mending needed as is bound to leave scars. You oughta fight jaybird-bare, so's to save your clothes. Skin'll heal a sight better'n cloth."

She discarded the trousers and bent to sponge the fist-sized purple patch on his upper thigh. At the touch of the moist cloth, he felt a stir under his summer-weight drawers; he focused his gaze on Janey Hand's low neckline, falling away even lower as she stooped over him, and the stir became a rigidity.

"Hey, now," Janey Hand said. "You're in no shape for them kind of doings. I better bring that right down." She slapped the wet cloth over his erection, which only strained the more in response.

Faro grabbed her beneath the arms and pulled her to him. "Hey!" she wailed indignantly. He felt the softness of her belly on his erection and the warm weight of her breasts pressing on him just below his ribcage. "You better—," she said, her voice muffled by his chest, but when she did not move to free herself in that first crucial second, he knew that the game was his.

Her stiffness eased. With slow deliberation, her head turned to one side, and her tongue darted out and caressed a scrape on his chest, moving back and forth until the crust of dried blood had been licked away. When she pulled herself loose, he did not try to hold her; he knew it was not a retreat.

Standing by the bed, she loosened her dress and shrugged out of it, then removed her cotton shift. Her breasts were high and full, with hardly a hint of a crease on their undersides; the nipples were pale rose and, he saw with satisfaction, puckered and erect—she wasn't just being accommodating, then. Her body was, like her face, a creamy pale gold, suggesting that she had a fondness for skinny-dipping out in some remote creek; normally, a woman would be close to dead-white except for her hands and face.

He pawed his drawers off and pushed them to the floor. Janey Hand studied him. "For a man that's took what you took from Horrible Henry, you're showin' a lot of liveliness."

"He didn't hit me there," Faro said.

"I suspect your prod's clearer as to what it's about than you are," Janey Hand said. "Believe I'll do my conversing with *it*. Rest of you's so chewed up or out of things, I could do you a injury."

She pulled a few pins from her coiled hair and let it fall over her shoulders, then knelt on the bed, parting Faro's legs. She wound her hair around his erection and slid it back and forth, tightening the golden coils around the base. Faro felt as if he had suddenly swelled to twice the size he had been.

"We got to get to know each other, him and me," Janey said dreamily. Slowly she rubbed the head of his penis across her forehead, then touched it delicately to her briefly-closed eyelids and slid it down one side of her nose. The light pull as it caught in one nostril was like nothing Faro had ever felt, and he had to make a severe effort not to come at that instant. She brushed it with her lips, exhaled a warm puff of air onto it, drew it down her chin and throat, touched it to each stiff nipple, half-circled the underside of each breast, then shifted on the bed, moving up until she straddled him.

"I guess we been introduced sufficient," Janey Hand said. "I'll do the movin', you stay still."

She lowered herself sweetly and slickly onto him, until the swollen redness of his erection was lost to his sight, and her damp pubic coils, soft and honey-colored, mingled with his own wiry blackness.

Then the rigid shaft, glistening now, came slowly into view as she raised herself with a little shuddering gasp that seemed to match the clenching flutter he could feel deep within her.

And then down again, then up, her breasts pendant above him, her hair drifting across his chest like cornsilk. She leaned to him, lightly, moistly, tonguing his blackened eye and the swelling knot of bone on his forehead; her breasts slid across the hair on his chest.

In spite of her orders against moving, he knew, could sense in his swollen maleness and the cradling flesh around it, when the time had come. He dug his fingers into her firm buttocks—registered but not minding the twinge of pain the effort cost his bruised hands—and arched upward beneath her, driving deep, until, despite the shielding of hair and flesh, their pubic bones slammed against each other, and he was right *there*, rubbing hard against her just where . . .

"*Aaahhohhh!*" Her head arched back, blue veins showing against the suddenly deep-rose neck and face, her teeth flashed in an involuntary, open-mouthed, mirthless grin; and Faro, coming and coming and *still* coming, was squeezed with a stunning series of near-ferocious contractions.

Janey Hand collapsed on him with an audible smacking sound as her wet flesh met his. She was like a marvelous, huge, hot poultice, soothing his aches. With a sense that his head was beginning to clear—and a profound feeling of gratitude that he'd been punched drunk enough to bring all this about—he recalled Evelyn Sutcliff's description of him as a living quilt. Was that time better than this? he wondered vaguely. Hard to tell, so different . . . Anyhow, this Janey's not a talker, one thing to the good.

That was his last clear thought before sleep claimed him. When he awoke, it was dark, and the girl was gone.

Chapter 7

Afternoon in the Goldroom was generally quieter than other times in the day or night. This day the sun was burning brightly outside, and the town lay somnolent in the hazy heat. Inside the saloon it was cool. The game was five-card stud.

Faro was seated at a table with a horse trader named Dummy Wilson, Hondo Jennings, a land speculator, Doc Hinderman, Cholly Wills, an old stove-up bronc-buster, and a stranger in town named George Brown.

Faro was cutting the game which had been dribbling along for a couple of hours when suddenly it came to life. Dummy Wilson was dealing and had caught an ace on the third card, his second being a six. Faro held two sixes exposed. All the other players had folded. On the first round the betting had been five dollars.

Faro was high with the sixes and he bet ten

dollars. Dummy raised to twenty. Faro called. He was watching Dummy closely. He knew that Dummy was figuring that if he, Faro had only two sixes he should have folded, since his own hand of six and ace showing looked like his hole card was an ace, giving him a pair. But Faro only called.

On the fifth card Dummy drew a nine. Faro caught a four.

Faro, of course, was just setting it up for the kill with three sixes. Dummy was clearly a dude; no intelligent player would have figured Faro had two pair—sixes and fours. Even a damn fool wouldn't draw to six, four. At the same time, if Faro had only two sixes he sure wouldn't call what looked like two aces in Dummy's hand and hope to draw out. Faro could just about read Dummy's mind; he was that close to him in concentration.

After the fourth card Dummy bet fifty dollars. Faro, hesitating a moment, called.

On the fifth card Dummy drew the second nine, making a six, an ace and a pair of nines showing. Faro drew a jack, and now had a pair of sixes, a four and jack exposed.

Faro realized that Dummy's second nine could have been dangerous except for the fact that two nines had been folded—one by Doc Hinderman and the other by the bronc buster. This made it dead sure that Dummy wasn't holding three nines. Faro figured he had a lock with his three sixes. He had bluffed Dummy into thinking he had only the two sixes which were showing.

Dummy had obviously made aces over nines. He bet one hundred dollars.

Faro threw in a hundred, and followed this with a hundred and fifty better.

"Raise you a hundred and fifty."

Dummy scratched his neck and looked at Faro's cards. Faro was reading it right along with him, his eyes right on Dummy's face and hands. Dummy, he knew, was figuring the jack, Faro's last card, had paired with the hole card, making jacks over sixes. This would account for Faro's boldness in betting the hundred and fifty. But, of course, Faro would never have drawn to a jack and six; he would have folded in the first place.

"I call," Dummy said at last.

Faro spread his hand. "Three sixes." And he pulled in the pot.

At this Dummy Wilson flung down his cards. There were tears in his eyes as he snarled, "You tricked me, God damn you!"

Faro didn't move a muscle. Then cool as spring water he said softly, "You tricked yourself, mister." He pocketed his winnings. "Gambling is for grown-ups."

As he walked back to the Chicago House he remembered how A.B. had taught him just that play he had used against Dummy Wilson. He had asked his father whether you always drew to small pairs if you had them backed up.

"If they are eights or less, I take only one card," A.B. had said. "Then if I don't make three right off I fold. It's a dude play to draw the limit to a small pair. If you don't catch something, you're licked. The betting gets too steep. But if you've got nines or better, then you can draw the limit; unless the play meanwhile shows I am beat."

Faro was just entering the hotel when Cole Herkimer's deputy, Harry Casebolt, came down the street. He was walking fast.

"Seen the marshal?" he asked Faro.

"Not today."

Harry Casebolt ran his hand over his face a couple of times fast and said, "That Texan, Hobart Maxwell, is down at the office looking like hell and raisin' hell and insistin' he see the marshal and right now. He is sore, I mean sore as a boil on a whore's ass."

Faro walked into the Chicago House wondering what was up. He had been standing at the bar only about fifteen minutes when Herkimer walked in. The marshal had clearly just come off a long ride.

"Your deputy was looking for you," Faro told him.

"Know what he wanted?"

"Said Maxwell was down at your office raising holy hell." Faro tapped the ash off his cigar so that it fell precisely into the cuspidor at his feet. "Didn't say what the wild hair up his ass was about."

Herkimer sniffed. "I'll go wash up first." A wry grin touched his face. "That was some wild-goose chase over to Tenant Wells, let me tell you." He downed his whiskey and disappeared.

In a few minutes he was back, looking refreshed and more at ease.

"Have another?" offered Faro amiably.

"Better not. I'll go see Maxwell. Then if you're still about, I'll call you on that drink."

Faro finished his bourbon and then started

upstairs to his room. It would be nice to take it easy for an hour. He was feeling extra good as a result of his beating Dummy Wilson.

He closed and locked the door behind him, a precaution he inflexibly took ever since the time an irate husband had burst in upon him and his errant wife while they were coiled in sexual festivities in Faro's bed. Faro had a hell of a time getting out of that one.

As he opened the leather case that held his advantage tools, a cloth pouch rolled out onto the bed, explaining why the case had felt bulkier than usual. Faro's heart stopped for a beat when he opened the pouch and saw what was inside. As he spilled the diamonds onto the bed there was no question in his mind as to where they had come from.

Chapter 8

It was no joke. It was no joke at all. What in hell were those damn diamonds doing in his room? And who had put them there? One thing was for sure, and that was that if they were found in his room, nothing he could possibly say would do any good. He'd be strung up from the nearest tree, and no mistaking that, by God.

Faro could hardly believe the evidence lying right there on the bed. Why? Obviously someone was trying to frame him—somehow. That was clear. He stood now, gazing out the window, his mind racing, trying to figure the angles, the options. Yes, that had to be it. Someone had planted the damn diamonds and someone was expected to find them—probably the law—right here in his room.

And right then and there, as though in answer to this frightful thought, who should he see striding along the street but Maxwell and Herkimer. They had that high-in-the-shoulders-and-chest look that meant they were dead set on hard business. Faro didn't have to guess what that business was. They were dead centered on the Chicago House, and there wasn't a moment to lose.

Where to hide the diamonds? His eyes suddenly fell upon the bottle of bourbon on the table beside his bed. Without giving it a second thought, he swept up the diamonds and tipped them into the bottle. The colorless stones vanished completely in the dark fluid.

But what about the pouch? Snatching it from the bed he dashed downstairs, out the back door and into the privy. In a second the incriminating pouch was deep down the hole.

Faro had just made it back to his room when Maxwell and Herkimer burst in without knocking—Maxwell in a rage, Herkimer apologetic for the intrusion. Then Faro saw the dried blood all over Maxwell's face.

"What happened to you?" he said.

"What happened to me!" roared the Texan. "Don't you know what happened to me, God damn you!"

"If I did I wouldn't be asking," Faro said icily. He was beginning to get properly fed up with the bullying Maxwell.

"You listen to me!" the Texan boomed.

"No, you listen to me, mister!" Faro's voice was as hard and cold as a gun barrel. "Who the hell do you think you are busting in here. Get your ass out before I throw you out. I am not taking any of your bluster!"

The big Texan stopped cold, surprise sweeping

over his face. He was obviously not accustomed to anyone talking to him like that.

Herkimer cut in at this point. "Blake, Maxwell got bushwhacked this morning on the way back to his herd. Got shot right out of the saddle, and the diamonds he was telling us about last night were taken. Luckily, he just got a scalp crease. But the bushwhacker must've figured he'd killed him."

"That murderin' sonofabitch has got to be someone who was at that dinner last night, Blake!" roared Maxwell, regaining some of his gall. "I demand that the marshal search your room. You were at that dinner, and by God, I want your room searched. I don't care whether you like it or not."

"Maxwell, I don't care whether you like it or not, but my room is not going to be touched by anybody."

"Blake, it would look real bad if you refused." Herkimer's tone was calm, but firm. And Faro saw the sense in what he was saying. He was a gambler; he was new in town; he had been at Evelyn Sutcliff's party. It would only throw heavy suspicion on him if he refused to allow the search.

"All right then."

"It is my duty," Herkimer said.

"I said go ahead."

It didn't take the marshal long to conduct his search. And he was thorough. Finally, Herkimer ran his hands over Faro, which irritated him mightily.

When Herkimer was finished Maxwell suddenly said, "I could sure use a drink." And his eyes were on the bottle of bourbon.

"Then you can damn well buy your own," Faro said.

Maxwell unexpectedly burst out laughing. "By God, Blake, you got balls, and I like that. The drinks are on me then." Then he said, "No hard feelings about this, but I had to be real sure."

"I will take a drink on you," Faro said, playing it real tight. There was no point in pushing things too far, he decided.

Later at the bar, after the Texan had left, Faro found Herkimer discouraged.

"It's a shitty job, Blake. You work your ass off and for peanuts. Half the time I'm bored to death. Half the time I'm busier'n a cat covering shit on a marble floor. Now with this Maxwell hullabaloo it could be big trouble."

"But you're in well with this town aren't you?" Faro said.

"With certain people. There's a big faction likes the Wild Bill type of marshal; Henry Mc-Cluskie, that type, who's always spreading himself on one thing or another."

It crossed Faro's mind to level with the marshal, but he knew that if he admitted to having the diamonds, there was no way an honest officer would be able to let it go at that. Herkimer would have to arrest him and hold him for trial, since Faro just had no reasonable explanation for the diamonds being in his possession.

Given some time maybe he could work out a way of getting the diamonds back to Maxwell without risking his own hide. But meanwhile he had to do something to protect himself. The bottle of bourbon was not the greatest hiding place for those gems. But for the present he could think of no other.

Faro was still pondering the problem when he opened his bank that evening and started to deal. His mood brightened at the sight of Janey Hand, though he noticed fleetingly that she did not seem her customary cheery self.

The play was not exciting, and he closed early, deciding on cards for the rest of the evening. But first he walked up to the bar to have a word with his favorite barmaid.

"What are you looking so glum for?" he asked as he picked up the bottle she placed before him.

"I want to talk to you."

"In my room?"

"Not that," she said glumly. "Buy me a drink, will you, and I can sit down for a few minutes." She looked at him with a kind of falling away in her eyes, and he was suddenly touched. "It's serious."

Faro picked up his drink and crossed to a table in a back corner of the room. In only a few minutes Janey joined him.

"Shoot," he said.

She was leaning slightly forward on the table, with her hand loose around her glass, her eyes looking down. When she looked up at him, he saw the tears.

"My brother Johnny." For an instant her voice broke, but she collected herself and went on. "He . . . he was shot. Last night. In Hide Park."

"How?"

"At the Alamo. He was playing cards. Someone just shot him." And Janey burst into tears.

Faro sat watching her as she vented her sorrow, her shoulders shaking as noiseless sobs wracked her body. He simply waited.

"Have you spoken with Herkimer?"

"That's just it. I asked him to find the killer. But he says he's too busy. He hasn't got but the one deputy, and they're trying to catch the stage bandits."

"So you want me to talk to him."

"Would you? Please?" She reached out and touched his hand. "Johnny, he was special."

"I'll do what I can. I don't promise anything."

"I've seen you talking with the marshal. I thought—"

"I'll do what I can." He reached across the table and touched the side of her face. Her cheek was wet with tears.

"Johnny didn't do anything. He wasn't even carrying a gun. This man just shot him."

"You don't have any notion who it was?"

"I don't know anything, only that Johnny . . . he is dead." And again the sobbing took her.

Faro waited for her to subside, not interfering, knowing that crying was the only thing she could do, that it was the best thing she could do.

Later, he wondered why the marshal had refused to look into the killing. The law, he decided, had wondrous ways of performing. Herkimer, after all, was one of the few really honest police officers he had ever encountered. And he had to admit he was surprised. But then, maybe he *was* too damn busy.

It was late when Marshal Cole Herkimer walked into the Goldroom on his evening rounds.

Faro had just pulled out of a game of five-card draw with deuces wild.

Tonight there was something different in the marshal, he saw. Herkimer had somehow changed. And in fact, he realized now that Herkimer had been different in his hotel room earlier. Faro had not really held that impression at the time, for he'd been so concerned with covering his tracks and getting the marshal and Maxwell away. But now, as he watched Herkimer tapping the side of his glass with his forefinger, he realized that it was a different man who sat before him. What was it? The frustration of not catching the bandits? Family troubles? Faro realized he knew nothing of Herkimer's background—where he came from, whether he had a wife, how long he'd been a marshal. All he knew was what had been mentioned at Evelyn Sutcliff's dinner party. That Herkimer had once located around Virginia City and Alder Gulch, where Henry Plummer had been sheriff. A thought suddenly began to form in his mind, but before it took concrete shape, the marshal cut in on him.

"Want to switch professions, Blake?"

Faro chuckled wryly at that. Then he decided on a frontal attack. Armed now with the casual moment of having a drink at a table, he brought up the subject of Janey Hand and her brother Johnny.

"Jesus, Blake. I just can't handle a killing in Hide Park. The place is a rat's nest. I've got my normal business of policing the main section of town."

"The tax-paying section."

"You said it. I let up one minute, and they start yelling. Hell, you heard them the other night. When are you going to catch the stage bandits? Have you got any fresh clues? and all that goddamn shit." He stopped suddenly, realizing he had let himself go. Then in a calmer voice he resumed. "Besides, that Hide Park bunch, it's understood around here that the section is a law unto itself."

"You're telling me the same you told Hand— you're busy."

"That's the size of it." He studied Faro a moment and then said, "How come you're so interested?"

"The lady is a friend, and she asked my help."

A knowing smile creased the marshal's face. "I see." He took a long swallow of his whiskey. "Look, I want to help. But I can't spare the time and I for sure don't have the manpower to look into this killing. But I've got an idea." He paused and took another drink.

Faro could not get over the thought that Herkimer was nervous, had something bothering him, in fact was not at all the calm, cool and collected man he had known until now. There seemed almost a kind of doom about him, as though he knew something bad was going to happen and was powerless to do anything about it.

"What's your idea?"

"Why don't you look into it? Wander over to Hide Park. Have a good look-see. You might turn up something a whole lot easier than I could since you won't be wearing a badge. Also, you're a known gambler, you're easy-going and you get

along with people. I think people might open up
to you—certainly more quickly than they would
to a lawman."

Faro smiled. "Never figured myself for a lawman, Herkimer." He laughed, his face wreathed
in good humor. "The idea appeals to me. I'll do
it." He held up his glass in a toast. "Here's to the
Masked Marshal!" And they both chuckled at
that.

"You bring in any sound evidence, I promise to
act on it." Now Herkimer leaned forward confid-
ingly and spoke in a softer voice, but his words
were insistent. "You might also keep eyes and
ears open for any sign of Maxwell's diamonds. I
tell you, Blake, I'm not so all-fired sure the thief
was one of the crowd at Mrs. Sutcliff's dinner."
He wagged his head. "There is something fishy
about that whole damn business with Maxwell."

And Faro told himself he couldn't have agreed
more.

"Blake, let me tell you I'm worried. That
Maxwell, if he spreads much more noise around,
I'm liable to be out of a job. I'm planning to get
married in the fall and I can't afford to be out of
work."

Faro must have looked his surprise for Herkimer said, "Keep it to yourself, about my getting
married. I shouldn't have said it, though I know
I can trust you."

"I thought you said you didn't want any more
trouble," Faro said lightly. Herkimer grinned at
that.

"I'm serious though. Like I told you, there are
a lot of people who favor the rip-roaring type of
gun-toting police officer. So they would take

advantage of anything that might make me look bad."

"I think you're in here pretty solid, if you ask me," Faro countered, "though you weren't asking me. I think you don't have anything to worry about. Hell, what more can you do?"

But with another part of himself Faro was thinking how strange that Herkimer was worried like that. He passed a few more comments with the marshal, and then Herkimer left.

It was around one o'clock when Maxwell came in. He had been drinking, Faro could see, but he didn't appear to be in an antagonistic mood. This changed swiftly, however, after he had joined the game. Faro was dealing five-card draw and won heavily.

"Blake, I hope you are not dealing seconds." Maxwell's voice fell like a piece of carrion onto the table. Nobody said anything.

"You have anything you can prove, Maxwell?" Faro said. "Or are you going to apologize? I don't take that from anybody."

There was a scraping of chairs as the other players swiftly withdrew, and Faro and the Texan sat facing each other.

Suddenly Maxwell slumped in his seat, his face twisted in pain. He lifted his hand and ran it twice across his face. His voice was low as he said, "Got me one helluva headache, Blake." He looked up and appeared surprised that the other players had deserted the table. Then: "I don't mind telling you I got it about figgered out who shot me. I can almost see the sonofabitch."

"What do you mean?" Faro leaned forward so he could hear better. There was no doubt in his mind that the Texan was leveling. He looked ashen, and his hands were trembling. "Maybe you need a drink," Faro said.

"Could stand it."

They stood up and moved to a corner table, and Faro brought over a bottle of whiskey and poured two drinks.

"You know," Maxwell said, "I saw him. But I can't quite remember. I figger as how maybe the shock of getting hit by that bullet in the head blanked me out. What do you think?"

"Could be. I have heard of such a thing happening." Faro spoke guardedly for he had no idea where the conversation would lead. He knew that Maxwell was quite capable of suddenly blowing. In view of this he kept his right hand close to the Reid under his broadcloth coat.

"I saw him, but I blanked out. I'm still blanked out. And yet—God damn this headache!—and yet I almost see him now. Shit, I hope I'm not losing my memory."

Suddenly he raised his head. He had been staring down at the table top while he spoke, but now he raised his head and glared at Faro.

"I am telling you, Faro, if that man turns out to be you when I do see him, I swear to Sweet Jesus I will skin you alive and pound you into beef jerky."

"I thought you had exonerated me after Herkimer searched me and my room," Faro said wryly.

"In a pig's ass!"

Faro said, "Better get your ass in bed. Maybe your memory will come back, not that I personally give a shit one way or the other." He took out a cigar and took his time lighting it. "I'm tired of listening to your shit, Maxwell."

"Fuck you, Blake."

"Glad you're in a better mood," Faro said, and he turned on his heel and walked out of the saloon.

He had decided that this was as good a time as any to take a sashay over to Hide Park.

Chapter 9

In the early years, one thousand head of cattle was considered a large herd, but in the seventies the herds often consisted of five, six thousand head. The size of the trail crew depended on the size of the herd. One or two herders to a hundred head of cattle was the usual rule. The trail hands were chosen with the greatest care. Each cowboy needed from two to six horses. Besides the herders, a trail boss, a cook, two horse wranglers who cared for the extra horses, several wagons, pack mules to carry provisions, and an abundant supply of firearms, saddles, lariats, blankets, short-handled whips, bedding, slickers, clothing and other personal belongings of the riders, made up the outfit.

Trail driving was no holiday trip. It was hard; it was very hard work and it was lonely. By the time those horny cowhands got anywhere near the town which would be the shipping point for the herd they were ready to rip the place apart. Which they often did.

Honeytown, on the border of the Indian Territory was no exception. And Hide Park, on the south side of the railroad track, and isolated from the main part of town, was not unique; it was just "more so."

The buildings in that raunchy community consisted of a dozen roughly-built wooden houses, two of which were dance halls. One dance house was kept by a man named Harry the Wizard; the other was under the direction of Alonzo Fold, a former undertaker. As some wag put it, Alonzo was continuing his life's work of dealing with bodies. They were thirty yards apart, and around them were other houses. The grass near the buildings was stubbed and yellow, and dim lanes had been worn by the feet of customers. At all hours of the night and on Sundays could be heard the music of the orchestras and the hippity-hop of the dancers. A bar was a definite part of each establishment, and it was mandatory that the dancers patronize it upon the conclusion of each dance. Drinks cost twenty-five cents each. The bar realized two dollars for each dance. But the bar enjoyed another patronage than that of the dancers; it was constantly besieged by a crowd of spectators who were always on hand to witness the wicked festivities.

Men continually crossed from one house to the other, occasionally to seek a change of music, but more often in search of a fresh partner. In one corner of each hall was a gaming table.

About a dozen girls were on duty in each dance house.

Here was paradise for the Texas cowboy. For no doubt about it, the chief business of Honeytown was trafficking in Texas cattle. Not less than two thousand drovers and buyers were in town that year. Cowpunchers could be seen everywhere: on the streets, in the gambling houses, in the saloons, and for sure in Hide Park's exciting establishments. Meanwhile, on the prairie adjoining the town, thousands of longhorns grazed.

Faro had it from Janey Hand that Horrible McCluskie was down in Hide Park singing a big brag, badmouthing Herkimer, and trying to get started as a pimp. Faro had wondered what McCluskie might have to do with Maxwell's diamonds. For sure, the big man had been seen in the Chicago House around the time of the action, and he could have planted the diamonds in Faro's room. But why would he? Sure, McCluskie had it in for him, but why would he take out his revenge in an action that would only spite himself? Why not simply take the diamonds? Planting them on Faro for revenge was a tremendous indulgence was how Faro looked at it. And yet, Faro still did not discount the possibility that McCluskie might have done just that, for over the years he had learned one very important thing about human nature. He had learned that the only thing you could trust in people, the one facet of human character that was always predictable, was that human beings were absolutely not predictable.

Faro paused just outside the Kitten Dance Hall, owned and operated by Harry the Wizard, just for a few moments to light a fresh cigar. Overhead, a handful of stars twinkled, and a slight breeze stirred, bringing a whiff of a nearby herd of cattle on the surrounding prairie.

Inside, the Kitten was alive with the wild jangle of piano, violins and banjo, accompanied by the scraping sound of heavy boots; and now and again, above the vibrancy of the stringed instruments, rose the "do-si-do" of the caller. Watching the scene Faro found himself comparing the Kitten to Annie Chambers' palatial quarters in Kansas City, the last house of pleasure he had visited. Annie ran probably the supreme cat house of the western world, with beautiful girls, and furnishings that put many a rich man to envy: the ornate mahogany staircase, the exquisite cut-glass mirrors, the thick red Brussels carpets. No, by God, the Kitten didn't hold a match to Annie's K. C. chambers. But it had its attractions, at least for Faro. He was always adaptable, and he loved the lively life whether it was in San Francisco, K.C., Denver, or in cowtowns such as Abilene, Ellsworth or Honeytown. It was the fun that counted; what the hell.

He saw quickly that all forms of gambling went, though keno was the most popular game. And the girls? The girls, so far as he could see, appeared quite passable. Yes, he was glad he had come, he decided, as he worked his way to the bar.

"Make it bourbon," he said to the bartender, a tall, completely bald-headed man named Clem.

Faro had not the slightest idea how to find out anything on the murderer of Janey Hand's brother; and in fact, while he had said he would try to help, he was not really too enthusiastic, for his real concern was with Maxwell's diamonds. Where would he dump them? Also down the outhouse hole? But that would be a terrible waste.

He had just taken a swallow from his glass when suddenly Horrible Henry McCluskie barged up beside him.

"Well, if it hain't our famous gambler!"

Faro studied the big man for a moment, checking for sincerity or guile, friendliness or hostility.

Then McCluskie said, "You handle your dukes pretty good. But you had me on a bad day. Next time I'll really clean yore clock for fair." He raised his glass. "Shit, what's done is done."

And Faro drank to that with considerable relief. He had no wish at all to go through another battle with Horrible Henry.

Suddenly he discovered a brilliant thought. Rather than resist or react to McCluskie, why not use him. Because, like everyone else, Horrible had his weakness, and Faro knew what it was.

"Still want to be a deputy, Henry?"

"How do you mean that?" And by the tone of his voice Faro could tell he had drawn the right card.

"I mean, I am in no position to promise anything, but I *am* looking for someone in Hide Park, and if you help me maybe I could help you."

"Looking for someone?"

"Yeah. Someone shot a cowboy name of Johnny couple of nights ago. I'm looking for him. You help me locate him, I'll turn him over to Herkimer, and I can put in a word for you there."

For a moment Faro thought he had said the wrong thing, for a string of obscenities flew from Horrible's wet mouth. It was like an eruption. "You're in with that sonofabitch are you!" he concluded. "Well, you better watch out. That's all I got to say. Cole Herkimer ain't what anyone thinks, ain't what you thinks neither; and you better watch your ass." He gulped his drink. "I say watch your ass with that boy!" Horrible leaned heavily on the bar, his lips pursed, his stetson hat pushed back on his head. "I could tell you plenty, by God. Plenty . . ." He seemed almost to be speaking to himself as he said those words, and Faro had to lean a bit to catch them. He was about to say something to get Horrible to speak further on the subject of Cole Herkimer when the big man suddenly straightened up.

He turned to face the room and now, with his elbows on the bar, he said, "Who you lookin' for here in Hide Park? Only real thing for a young whippersnapper like yourself to be huntin' would be pussy." He cocked his head at Faro and winked. "How you doin'? Been gettin' much, have you lately?"

"My share," Faro said with a smile. "I told you who I was looking for; feller that killed the cowboy named Johnny Hand. It was right here maybe, or over to the Alamo, I don't know. But you must have heard something."

"You say you might smooth it between me an' Herkimer?"

"That's what I said. I said I'd try leastways."

Horrible McCluskie broke into a sudden grin. "What I'd truly like you to do is show me how to slicker some of these here dudes with a deck of cards."

"Like for instance?"

"Like how to win at poker. I note you win pretty steady, and nobody sees you second dealing or anything like that. Only thing is, I *know* you have got to be pulling something, Blake. I know that." His grin broadened. "You teach me, I'll see what I can come up with. Fair deal?"

Faro considered it. It was out of the question to show McCluskie anything to do with a rigged deck or a holdout, for the news would be all over Kansas before you could scratch your own ass. But he could show him how to play.

"Tell you what, Henry. I won't teach you how to cheat, because I don't know how. And also it's against the rules. But I *will* teach you how to play a straight game and win. How's that? Are you on to that?"

"I'm on. But you got to show me good." And his big forefinger reached down and tapped the handle of the big Hogleg strapped to his side. "I wouldn't want me to keep my side of the bargain and you not keep yourn."

"Nor would I," Faro said wryly, and bid Horrible adieu.

The moment he walked into his room at the Chicago House he knew someone had been there. It didn't take any great skill to find out why. A quick shake of the bottle of bourbon revealed that the diamonds had again disappeared.

Chapter 10

The other shacks in Hide Park were in even worse shape than the two dance halls. Faro wondered what kept them standing, and he felt this especially when he walked into the rude structure that harbored Horrible Henry McCluskie.

Through Janey Hand he had received a message that Horrible wanted to see him, and he reasoned that it was in relation to Johnny the cowboy's killing.

Faro had not yet been inside one of the Hide Park "residences," but he knew that none could be more tenuous, small or downright filthy than the one-room shack where he found McCluskie.

The giant was seated on the one chair in the room, a backless affair. He was in the process of cleaning and cutting his fingernails with a buffalo skinning knife. Those nails were like coal shovels, Faro reflected as he took the only other seat, an upended wooden box. In a corner of the room was a filthy buffalo robe, on which lay a bottle of booze and some of Horrible's personal articles; for instance, a cartridge belt, something resembling clothing, possibly a shirt, and a single boot. The only other appointments were a coal-oil lamp, the chimney of which was black with soot, and the battered table on which it stood.

"Got some news for ya," the giant said without looking up as Faro sat down carefully.

"I'm listening."

"Our deal still on?" McCluskie looked up, cocking an eye.

"Still on."

Horrible Henry sighed, leaned back and suddenly flung the buffalo knife into the wall of the shack. So flimsy was that wall that the heavy knife, under the power of McCluskie's arm, almost split the wood and passed on through. Faro realized that the boards were separated so that air came through and he wondered what it must be like in the winter months.

McCluskie nodded in the direction of the two dancing establishments. "He is yonder. Goes by the name of Crawford Hinds."

"The name is familiar."

"Runs the dice game at the Alamo. He's crooked as a parson's heart in a whorehouse after he's had his licks."

"I've seen him." Faro nodded as he remembered. "Thin, with long, greasy hair to his shoulders, and long hands, good for palming dice."

McCluskie grinned. "That's the size of him."

"You sure it was him?"

"Sure as I am Alonzo Fold's raking in a fortune, the goddamn flesh peddler." And Mc-Cluskie laughed aloud in admiration of the enterprise of the Alamo's proprietor.

"But do you have any witnesses?" Faro insisted.

"About twenty people seen him do it. Shot that poor lonesome cowboy right there." He wagged his big head. "Shit."

"But the point is, will any of them testify?"

McCluskie spat toward the far corner of the room at a coal bucket Faro had not noticed, and which was already flecked with a liberal amount of brown spittle. "Reckon more than likely not, 'less they don't want to die of old age."

"So what good is that?"

"Mister, you asked me to find out who killed the cowboy. And I done same. Hell, Blake, half the damn saloon seen him do it."

"So I'll tell Herkimer."

"Fat lotta good that'll do you."

Faro paused over that one, remembering how Herkimer had insisted that there be witnesses who would testify. He stood up.

"I'll be back later," he said. "I'll go talk to the marshal. It's his business now."

"Don't you forget our deal, Blake." The words were underscored in Faro's mind as he left the shack.

Twenty minutes later Herkimer, confronted in his office with the news, merely said, "How can we prove it?"

"That's not my business," Faro said. "You going to make an arrest?"

"On what grounds? Suspicion? You know that

without witnesses I'll just have to let the sonofa-bitch go."

"But twenty people saw him do it."

"Fine, but who will testify? Blake, I know Hinds. And everyone in Hide Park knows him. Anybody opens his mouth on what happened, Hinds will cut his balls off. I mean that literally.

"So there's nothing you can do."

"Crawford Hinds is not your ordinary killer. I know him. I have known him a long time. He . . . used to hang around a place where I was once. There was this old prospector, Clubfoot Bill. Bill was more drunk than usual one time and made the mistake of spooking Crawford's horse. You know what that snake Hinds did?"

"Killed him."

"And then he skinned him."

"Holy shit!"

"I wouldn't be able to hold him an hour. Then, he'd more than likely run amok. He's that kind. I know." Herkimer stopped abruptly and seemed to be thinking. "I know . . . the type," he said. And Faro saw a strange look on his face.

It was evening when Faro returned to the McCluskie residence. The sun had left the sky, but it was still warm, and there was still a certain light even though two or three stars were out. The music from the Alamo and the Kitten fell into the soft air, mingling with the smell of a nearby herd. As he passed the Kitten the side door suddenly burst open, and a cowboy staggered out, grappling with his fly, stopped and almost fell; then, swaying on his feet while he urinated, he began to sing at the top of his voice.

Glad somebody's happy, Faro said to himself and he walked into McCluskie's shack without knocking. The Horrible one was still there, this time cutting his toenails with the buffalo knife. It was an event Faro would as soon have missed, for he couldn't imagine when McCluskie had last taken a bath or washed his feet. Quickly, he lighted a cheroot in an effort to wipe out the stench that gripped his nostrils.

This time McCluskie threw the skinning knife into the floorboards. Then, reaching over to the buffalo robe, he groped until he found two glasses which, with the bottle of whiskey, he placed on the table.

"A little liquid to honor our agreement," he said. Then, squinting at Faro he said, "I can see how far you got with our honest and upright marshal."

Faro managed to clean his glass somewhat, to the great amusement of McCluskie.

"Like all gamblers, you are that persnickety." He grinned wickedly. "Shit, you didn't really think Cole Herkimer was gonna go out and capture Crawford Hinds did ya?" And he threw back his head and roared.

Faro had the distinct feeling that he was getting into something he didn't want, and that something involved the marshal of Honeytown. All along now, McCluskie had been dropping hints, placing snide remarks, putting out suspicions on Herkimer's character; and he wondered what that added up to. Suddenly he remembered something. He remembered the evening at Evelyn Sutcliff's when he had noticed the shadow passing over Herkimer's face at the mention of Alder Gulch, and he remembered his conversation with Herkimer in the Goldroom when he had playfully, or ruefully, offered to switch professions with Faro. Both times Faro had the distinct impression that there was something in Herkimer's past.

Suddenly he said, "You knew Herkimer from the old days, huh." He put it as a statement, as though he knew it to be so.

McCluskie, who had not been slow to sample the rotgut from the bottle and indeed seemed to caress it with his tongue, a smile of pleasure on his face, said, "I know Cole Herkimer from—" And he stopped suddenly, his smile breaking into a wicked grin. "I'm keeping all that tightly corralled, mister. You stop askin' me all them questions."

"I wasn't asking you anything," Faro said easily. "I just was talking about things Cole had mentioned here and there."

"Yeah? Like what?"

"Like he knew you . . . in the old days."

"You're lyin'." McCluskie was suddenly sober. "All I've been saying, Blake, is that Herkimer won't pull in Crawford for that shooting. And here you go building up a big story on something or other."

Faro stood up suddenly, realizing he had played his card too soon. And yet, he knew he had been right, too. Herkimer and McCluskie had known each other in the past. Not that in itself there was anything wrong in that.

"I knowed Cole over in Boise, Idaho; but not close. Just he was there and me too. Like that."

But Faro was still not satisfied. For the moment he decided to drop it.

McCluskie said, "Sit down, finish your drink. Have another."

Faro had no wish to drink any more of the

forty-rod rotgut that McCluskie called whiskey. He said, "I'll give you your first lesson." He rubbed his hands together. "Only trouble is one thing."

"What's that?"

"Thing is you are not very fast with your hands. And that's what's—" He stopped abruptly at the sight of the big blue Navy Colt pointing right at his belly button. He had never seen anyone draw that fast.

"You were sayin' . . . ?" Horrible McCluskie's grin was real mean.

"I get your point, Henry; but I'm talking about cards, dice, being fast that way. I'll show you what I mean. Put that thing away."

Facing McCluskie across the rickety table, Faro took out a deck of cards and swiftly dealt.

"Now, I have got a hole card not showing, and an ace showing. My hole card is also an ace." He turned the ace face up to show Horrible. "And you have got a king in the hole and a king showing. We both have two other cards, because this is five-card draw, making it four cards each. That doesn't matter because we're just practicing. The point is I have got aces over your kings, and there's one card coming to each of us." He put down his cigar. "Got it?"

"I got it."

"Now look. I am dealing, but I deliberately hold the deck in such a way that you can't help but see your last card will be another king. That means two kings showing and a king in the hole which, in a real game, I would not know was there. So you will have three kings. Right?"

"Right!"

"You see that king all right?"

"Sure do." Horrible Henry was grinning with excitement.

"So watch now. We bet. I have raised you, and you cover. We've got a couple of thousand in that pot." Now watch very carefully." And with a little twitch of his left hand Faro flipped a queen over McCluskie's cards.

"What the hell . . . I saw a king!"

"Wait and be quiet."

Setting the deck down with his left hand, Faro reached out with his right and took for himself the king from the top of the deck just where it had been all along.

"Christ almighty!" cried the flummoxed Mc-Cluskie.

"Are you learning something?"

"Shit, Blake. It takes two people to watch you. One to see you start your play and the other to see you finish it!"

"What I am showing you is that you need speed, accuracy, and above all nerve. That's what you have to learn. The tricks alone don't mean a thing."

He stood up and put away the cards.

McCluskie sat there wagging his head in admiration. He just couldn't believe what had happened right before his eyes.

"I heard you dropped a bundle or two over in that dice game Hinds is running."

"That sidewinder."

"I'm going to show you how to get even. But it could get real hairy. You follow me?"

Horrible Henry tapped the six-gun at his right side. "I am sidin' you with both hands," he said and tapped the gun at his left hip. "You get that slimy bastard and I am with you." He grinned. "You know, that little Janey Hand has a great pair of tits."

As always, the crowd around the dice table at the Alamo was thick. The crowd pressed in on the players and Hinds, who was running the game, had to keep telling them to move back, to give the rollers room.

Faro had watched Hinds before. He was a mean one, no doubt about it; lean as whang leather and dangerous as snake poison. He had little eyes, and they were always looking, like two ferrets, missing nothing. His most impressive trait from Faro's point of view was his reflexes. He was quick, like a striking rattler. Faro had already studied Hinds' manner of play, knew that he threw in tops, palming the flats, then switching again as the situation demanded. In his vest pocket Faro carried a pair of tops, bought for twenty dollars from Grandine, and along with them a set of identical flats or straight dice. With these he had practiced assiduously, changing the dice like lightning so that now they were the flats, now the tops, with the spots so placed on them that no seven-combination could ever be thrown.

After watching the game for a while, Faro edged in close to the table, with McCluskie right beside him. When Faro got the dice, Hinds covered a couple of his throws with large bets, losing one and winning the other. When Faro passed the dice Hinds came out with a nine. He immediately offered to borrow on the six-ace draw for five hundred.

"On nines and fives I always bet on the make," Faro said.

"I'll make it for five hundred."

"Make it for a thousand," Faro said, and he pulled out a stack of bills, peeled off the amount and shoved it into the pot.

A tight grin cut across Hinds' face as he called; then threw the dice.

Faro reached out and picked up the dice, and as he threw them back to Hinds he said, "Two thousand you don't make it."

Hinds counted out the money while the crowd around the table fell silent in front of the drama that had developed. Hinds threw, bumping the dice hard against the table railing. They spun before settling. It was the six-ace, and Crawford Hinds' face turned white under his hairy jowls. Even his forehead and nose seemed to whiten.

When he straightened up, his right hand moved toward the edge of the table. "I'm giving you a chance to draw," he said. "You switched dice."

"What makes you think that?" Faro asked innocently. "Do you mean your dice were tops and couldn't make a six-ace?"

"You sonofabitch."

"I am not armed," Faro said. He reached forward and picked up the dice and turned them in his hands. "They look like straight dice to me." And he threw them to Hinds, just as the latter's hand moved below the table. At that same instant, Faro's own hand streaked to the Reid under his coat. But Horrible Henry Mc-Cluskie was quicker than either of the dice players.

The surprise on Crawford Hinds' face was

complete as he took two slugs in the heart and fell dead across the table, his face covering the dice that Faro had tossed at him.

"Justice triumphs," said McCluskie as two men carried the corpse out of the room.

"Justice, my ass," said Faro. "It was those dice I tossed at him that triumphed." But he knew that without McCluskie there he wouldn't have made it.

Later, over a drink, Horrible Henry said, "Tell me what happened. What are tops?"

"Crawford threw his nine," Faro explained. "Then he switched to tops so he could no way throw a seven, a six-ace. That's when we started betting. He didn't figure on me palming his tops and slipping in a pair of flats." He sighed. "And besides, he should have remembered that a handful of dice isn't any help when you're trying to draw on a man."

"I don't get you. He didn't catch those dice when you threw them. He let them fall."

"But he was going to, and that distracted him for a second. Otherwise, for all your fast draw, McCluskie, it would have been us they carried out." And he smiled, watching it sink into Horrible Henry McCluskie.

Chapter 11

"What do I know about Maxwell?" McCluskie belched loudly, raking Faro with the odor of onions and old tobacco. He was indeed very drunk and had fallen into the chair when they sat down at the table in the Kitten. "I know about Maxwell. He . . . he . . . I know . . . I dunno. I don't know nothin'."

This contradictory utterance puzzled Faro, and he asked, "What do you mean? What the hell do you mean, you know and you don't know?"

"I mean what I says." Horrible had been leaning on the table with his elbows and now he let his forearms fall like trees onto the wooden top. The table cracked under the assault, but remained standing.

"Shit," said Faro. The room was crowded.

Earlier, Faro had reported to Janey Hand on what had happened at the Alamo, and in her elation she had stood them both a round of drinks. "But what do you really mean?" Faro insisted.

"Whyn't you ask Cole Herkimer? Whyn't you ask old King Cole?"

"Ask him what?"

"Ask him about the diamonds." He suddenly spat a thick streak at a cuspidor that stood nearby, but missed, and it splattered the floor. "Huh . . . ask him about the bandits."

"About the bandits?"

McCluskie laughed loudly at Faro's puzzlement. "Think I am funning, do ya?"

"What about Maxwell?"

"Same thing, my boy. Same thing. And you can bet your bottom dollar or yer ass, whichever is more important." He belched swiftly again and resumed. "Ole King Cole." He chortled, reeking across the table into Faro's face. "Ole King Cole was a merry ole sole." He roared. "A merry ole sole was Cole." He sniffed. "Cole rhymes with hole; with asshole. A merry ole asshole was ole Cole." And his face disappeared into his beard as he folded in a huge laugh, shaking, tears pouring from his eyes, slapping the table and almost spilling the drinks; finally gasping into a fit of coughing. It was several moments before he came wheezing back to the conversation with Faro. He sat there wagging his head, drumming his fingers along the side of his glass of whiskey.

Faro tried another trick. "I hear talk there's going to be an election for marshal. You figuring on running, Henry? How do you see your chances?"

"You can let Herkimer do the running," answered McCluskie. "Me, I'll just sashay my big ass into that there job. When I tell all I know about—"

"McCluskie!" The new voice cut into the room like a knife.

Suddenly everything stopped. There had been a sort of background hum in the room, loud but not insistent, and now this abruptly ceased. The silence was ominous to Faro; it seemed louder than the noise had been.

The room was without the slightest movement. Heads turned to look at the tall, broad-shouldered marshal. Now, those who had been near McCluskie and Faro moved away. Everyone was aware of how the big man had been badmouthing Herkimer over the past few days. Everyone knew it could go no further, that this was the confrontation.

Cole Herkimer, dressed neatly in dark broadcloth, was the center of everyone's attention in that room. In that rough crowd, and with the exception of Faro, he stood out like a piece of new money. There was no question in Faro's mind that the next few moments were Cole Herkimer's decision.

Slowly, Herkimer put a long thin cigar in his mouth and drew on it. From beneath the wide, hard brim of his black hat his light blue eyes bore into Horrible Henry McCluskie. Herkimer was silent. Presently, he removed the cigar with easy grace, tapped the ash, his eyes not leaving McCluskie.

When he spoke, his words were precise, clear, almost clipped. Faro could understand why some people in Honeytown thought he was English.

"I am interrupting your conversation, McCluskie, before you make a jackass of yourself and get into real trouble." And his right hand moved slightly. As his eyes flicked to Faro and returned to McCluskie there was a mild stirring in the room which quickly subsided. Faro took the moment to remove himself from any possible line of fire.

McCluskie turned his head now to stare with clouded eyes at the source of that cold voice. Slowly he rose to his feet.

"Behave yourself, Henry," Herkimer said.

Suddenly McCluskie's hand snaked to one of his holstered guns. It was halfway out of its holster when Cole Herkimer had him covered. "I wouldn't, Henry."

Horrible Henry McCluskie stopped cold, the blood rushing to his face, and now Faro could see the sweat on his forehead and cheeks as he let the six-gun drop back down into its holster.

"Drop your hand away from your gun," Cole Herkimer said. "I mean right now."

Without a word McCluskie let his hand fall to his side. Cole Herkimer's weapon stayed right on him for a moment, and then, swift as a wink, it was back in its holster.

A high, nervous laugh broke from someone in the back of the room, and McCluskie spun toward the sound.

"Stinkin' bunch of yeller rats!" he shouted. "Ain't a man in the whole yeller bunch of ya!"

He stood glaring at the sea of faceless faces, knees bent, his great head dark with his tremendous fury. "Yeller rats!"

Maybe it was the fact that nobody said anything that did it. Horrible Henry squatted on the floor, stood erect, kicked at some dust. His voice rose even higher, a shrill whine, piercing every corner of that intense room.

"Ain't never met Cole Herkimer!" The voice was almost a scream. "Ain't seen, ain't knowed! The respectable Cole Herkimer. Hah!" He scratched under his arms furiously. "You don't know him; you don't know him." He stabbed his finger at faces in the crowd. "None of you dumbass shitheels knows the real Cole Herkimer. But I know him. I *know* Cole, ole King Cole. 'Cause I am big Henry McCluskie!"

The voice cut like the edges of jagged tin as he kicked the floor, while the sweat poured from his great flat cheeks. "I'm big Henry McCluskie, an' I kin outfight, outshoot and, by golly, outfart any outlaw in this here territory. Courtesy of Cole Herkimer, 'course, that is . . ."

"McCluskie!" Cole Herkimer's voice was a knife. At the slash of it the giant faced the marshal of Honeytown full on, his right hand slipping toward his gun.

Just slightly, Cole Herkimer raised his voice. "I ask all of you to take note," he said, and his voice was as cool and clear as new ice. "This man has done injury to my name and reputation."

"I take note, Marshal Herkimer," said a man named Dutch Tilly. And Faro felt everything inside himself come together.

Cole Herkimer faced Horrible Henry McCluskie, whose hand now rested on the butt of his six-shooter. "Go on, Henry." And the marshal's elbow moved slightly so that the skirt of his coat would not interfere.

Instantly, the drunken giant was sober. "No," he muttered. "No. Hell, I wouldn't fight you, Cole. You boys, you know I wouldn't fight Cole Herkimer, not the marshal."

"Go ahead," Herkimer said, and his voice was flat as a rock.

Horrible Henry looked helplessly into the crowd, but no one said anything; no one met his eyes.

Suddenly someone sneezed, and a chair scraped on the floor. With a great sigh McCluskie went for his gun. The movement of his hand was stopped by a blast that brought him to his knees. His hands clutched his side while Cole Herkimer looked at him quietly from behind his Deane & Adams revolver.

"Cole!" McCluskie screamed. "I ain't on my feet!"

Casually, with his cigar still in his mouth, Cole Herkimer fired. McCluskie collapsed by a large brass cuspidor, not upsetting its contents, however.

The marshal of Honeytown, Kansas, walked over and nudged the squirming man with the toe of his boot. "He is not dead, only wounded. I didn't shoot to kill," he said. "Some men, carry him to the jail. Then get Doc Grimsman. McCluskie is under arrest."

As Herkimer turned to leave, he saw Faro and smiled. "I believe I told you Hide Park was an interesting attraction," he said.

But the humor fell a little flat for Faro, for he was remembering some of the things Horrible Henry had intimated about Herkimer. Hell, who *was* Cole Herkimer. Who was he really? And did he really know more than he was letting on about Maxwell's diamonds?

Chapter 12

All day Faro waited for news on Horrible Henry. The word was that McCluskie might have caught a bad one and was on his way to becoming a permanent resident of Honeytown, Kansas. On the other hand, it was opined that McCluskie would recover. Faro wondered why Herkimer had insisted he be put in jail, and not carried to Doc Grimsman's office directly where, clearly, he would be more comfortable, and would have easier access to medical attention. Was it so Horrible wouldn't talk? But about what?

In the evening, when Faro stopped by to see Horrible, the big man said, "He's as feerd of me as me of him." Herkimer had been out of earshot, in his office adjoining the jail, but McCluskie had not particularly lowered his voice—as though he didn't care whether he was heard or not, Faro thought.

The visit was short, and Faro wondered why he gave a damn what happened to Horrible Henry. There was something he couldn't help liking about the big bully and braggart, he supposed. At the same time, his curiosity over Herkimer was growing rapidly.

He had returned to his room at the Chicago House and was just getting ready to walk over to the evening festivities at the gaming tables when there was a knock at the door. To his great surprise who should walk in but Hughie "You Lose" Lewis.

"Well, I will be a horned-out toad if it ain't the old Texan hisself!" roared Faro, imitating what he figured to be a broad Texas accent. True or not, his effort was good enough to almost bring "You Lose" to the floor with laughter.

"How you doin', gambler?"

Lewis was all bone it seemed. He looked as though his skin had simply been laid over his skeleton to keep out the rain. Faro sometimes had the feeling that "You Lose" wouldn't really be able to move without rattling.

"I'm doing just fine," Faro said, returning to more or less pure Kentuckian. "What are you doing in this beautiful town?"

"I have just rid in with two thousand head and sold the critters for top dollar; an' Hughie Lewis is rarin' to go. Want to set up that game with you for tomorrer night."

"You're on."

"Got to make the early train next mornin' for Denver, so the session will have to be short."

"Good enough. But what's going on in Denver?"

"Silver. I got me some investment in a silver mine." He grinned at Faro. "Real, genuine, bona fide silver mine."

"And what's on for tonight?"

"Dip my wick, by Jesus. What the hell you think. I been on that fuckin' trail from hell to breakfast and back. Shit, I'm ready to eat it!"

They chortled as Faro poured. Then, holding high their tumblers, "You Lose" said, "Here's to the hole that never heals; the more you tickle it, the better it feels."

"By God, I'll drink to that."

It was good seeing "You Lose"; the Texan brought life wherever he went. A man in his seventies . . . you'd have thought he was fifty. Spry as a broomtail in the spring, and horny as a longhorn in a herd of heifers.

"One last one," Faro said, tipping the bottle.

"You're a good man, Faro Blake. But I am going to whip your ass tomorrow night." "You Lose" held his glass high. "I want to make a toast," he said.

"Go ahead."

"In the words of the immortal Horace Greeley: 'Go west, young man.'" He took a drink and held his glass high again. "And in the words of the immortal Hugh Q. Lewis: But, young man, don't be a horse's ass and stay there."

Faro found the Goldroom more crowded than usual, or at any rate it seemed so; but the play was good. He pulled in a good winnings for the evening, and he was feeling in good fettle as he walked home. The night was fresh, there was a half moon high in the sky, and the stars were brilliant. For a moment he toyed with the thought of having a last drink in the bar of the Chicago House, but decided against it and mounted the stairs to his room.

He was there only long enough to take off his coat and boots when there was a knock at the door. Wondering if it was "You Lose," returned from his bout down in Hide Park, he opened hoping to see his friend, for the voice that answered his call through the door did, in fact, have a Texas accent, though muffled.

But his visitor was a complete stranger. It was a fairly short figure, underneath a wide stetson hat, wearing chaps, a tooled vest, while a cigarillo accounted for the cloud of smoke that rose from beneath the wide hat brim toward the ceiling.

"What can I do for you, stranger?"

Suddenly the stranger's hand swept up and removed the hat to reveal a great spill of golden hair. It was Evelyn Sutcliff.

"What the hell . . ." said Faro, a smile of pleasure on his face as he stepped back into the room.

Evelyn followed him in and closed the door.

"What are you doing here?" Faro felt as though his question was indeed a foolish one, but it seemed necessary to say something.

"I came to see you. Do you mind?"

"Sure not. But why the disguise?"

"You can figure that out."

He locked the door behind her, and she moved to the bed and sat down.

"It looks good," Faro said, appraising her costume. "I like men fine, as men," Faro said.

"And women as women. I got strong notions that there is different ways of dealing with them."

"Men for fighting, women for fucking, is that it?" Evelyn Sutcliff said. In her male attire and cascade of blonde hair, she bore an unnerving resemblance to General George Armstrong Custer; but the ambiguous appearance made her blunt language a little less strange and, for some reason, made it possible to talk to her more candidly.

"It's not the whole of it, but that'll do for a rough sketch," Faro said.

"I saw you fight," Evelyn Sutcliff said.

"Didn't see you there."

She smiled thinly. "I was at the far edge of the crowd. A woman in my position gets to calculate pretty closely where to be at every kind of doings. A prizefight—I shouldn't be there at all. But it's a major event for the town, so, as the banker, I can't stay completely aloof. Now, up front, the only women are Hide Park girls and some of the better-class whores; so on the fringes, that's the place for Banker Mrs. Sutcliff. I wanted to talk to you afterward, but you somehow vanished."

"Took some hurts in the ring needed seeing to," Faro said. "All mended now." He would have bet ten double eagles that Evelyn Sutcliff had seen him stagger away with Janey Hand, and that she would never in any way refer to it—at least, any more than she had with that crack about the up-front women spectators. "What did you want to talk about?"

"What it felt like, fighting that is."

"It felt like hitting and getting hit," Faro said. "That's what there is to it."

"You know better than that," she said, "and so do I, for all that, I haven't been in a fight since Parvela Towson and I pulled each other's hair out in handfuls and scratched each other's faces when I was in seventh grade. But I remember what that felt like. And I remember what it felt like when I turned down Pete Rayburn for an extension on his mortgage and sold his place off at auction. He'd been mouthing off about women bankers and how I couldn't add two and two before he came to me, and, when I broke him, it was like your hitting McCluskie for the last time—or so it seemed to me."

Her intensity made Faro uneasy. "I'm a fighter," she went on, looking past him. "Business, living, they're contests for me—I'm not alive unless I'm fighting. The strange part is, in business you can win all the way, just like in the prize ring. Living, you have to just not *quite* win; you have to keep the one you're fighting with *still* fighting, all the way. And that means he has to be strong enough to counter you, but not so strong he can beat you."

Faro suspected that, whatever had taken the late Mr. Sutcliff off the scene, his widow regarded him as one who had not come up to scratch in her view of the prize ring of life. He wondered whom she'd been sparring with recently, then got a sudden sinking feeling as he realized that he seemed to fill the specifications. She was some electrifying lady, all right, but . . .

"I could fight *you*," she said, confirming his apprehensions.

"Not like I did with Horrible Henry," Faro said. "I tell you, for no reason other than my experience, a woman's not as smart as a man, or as brave—even, come to that, as mean. But you got to reckon with musculature, which is different. A man has got more than a woman has or whatever it is in his biceps and so on that makes him able to hit hard and take hard hits."

"They handicap for weight in races," Evelyn Sutcliff said, staring at him with bright eyes. "You give me a fair handicap, Mr. Blake, and I could show you something. How about I get to punch, you get to slap open-hand?"

"That's the—"

Evelyn Sutcliff cut off his "—craziest thing I ever heard of" with a brisk "—Way to do it, right?"

Faro was never quite sure what he had agreed to or how he had done so, but he suddenly found himself stripped to the waist, facing Evelyn Sutcliff, who had doffed everything but her breeches, with his open hands raised, as were her clenched fists. She danced up and down in a creditable imitation of a pugilist, setting her breasts into bewildering motion.

"Hey, now . . ." he said softly, then, *"shit!"* as her left fist caught him on the underside of the jaw.

"This ain't—*blf!*" Her raised right hooked into the still-bruised soft flesh under his ribs. "Hah!" He relished the sting in his palm as he slapped her in the side, then felt a sudden shame. Whatever her tastes, Mrs. Sutcliff was, after all, a lady—a *woman*. He revised the thought as she sank a left, knuckle-deep, into his midriff, keening—and it wasn't fitting for him to be—with pain as she drove an elbow into his throat!

From there on, it got rough.

Both parties kept to the stated agreement, but where Mrs. Sutcliff punched and where Faro slapped would have raised the Marquess of Queensberry's eyebrows. There came a moment when he had her pinned against the wall, sweat-slicked chest compressing full breasts, his left hand immobilizing her right, his right hand squeezing her chin. "Okay, you give up?" he said hoarsely.

"Give up what?" Her free hand snaked under the waistband of his drawers and clutched. "One twist, and you're a steer, Mr. Blake."

He threw back his head and laughed. "Why, then, we'd both lose what all this is over, wouldn't we?"

He flung her hands away, then grabbed her behind the knees and overset her so that she slammed to the floor, and wrenched the drawers off, freeing himself from his own undergarments, then plunging into her with an impact that drew a whistling grunt and a squeal of delight.

The acrid smell of the anger of combat mingled with the musky scent of lust as he rode her harder and harder, more brutal and uncaring and yet, in a way, he realized, more satisfying— than he had ever let himself be with a woman, up to the explosive finish line.

Were they to come and lift me up tenderly and take me away and put me on a scale now, he thought dimly, I believe I'd prove out at thirty-eight pounds or so. Mrs. S.—that I'm spraddled out on and like to be so awhile, as my bones have seemingly turned to jelly referred to me as a quilt some time back; I doubt I'd make more than a summer sheet, right now.

"You're a fighter, too," she mumbled from beneath him. "Match for me . . . you and me . . . we both could lose, 'cause up against each other, we'd both win . . . can't do better than that. So that's what we can do."

Mrs. Sutcliff's statement was not entirely coherent, but Faro caught its drift well enough. He could share the life, the fortune and the incredibly inventive body of this magnificent woman . . . *if* he would hang around to do it. Honeytown, Kansas, could be his home, and Evelyn Sutcliff his woman—make that *wife;* nothing more informal than that could exist outside of Hide Park.

Faro rolled away from her. What he had to say didn't fit well with being still inches deep in the woman who had to hear it. Then again, the gesture itself went a good way toward conveying the message. "If you want to think of people as plants," he said, "there are those that have roots. And then—"

Evelyn Sutcliff brought her hand down impatiently between her legs in what might have been a punishing slap or gesture of self-comfort. "Oh, suffering saints, a goddamn tumbleweed! I *would* set myself on one of them, wouldn't I? A goddamn *cabbage*, a goddamn *loco* weed, now a copper-bottomed, triple-riveted *tumbleweed!* Wouldn't you think I could get a fucking *oak* tree, or even a cottonwood? Oh, you bastard, that's it, get out; go on, get out."

"Ah . . ." Faro said. "My room."

Evelyn Sutcliff expressed her general opinions of Faro, his room, the Chicago House, the State of Kansas and the Union of which it was part, the great globe itself and the universe as she flung herself into her male disguise and stamped out of the room.

That was some jangling, Faro reflected, composing himself for sleep. But one thing, it's not one of your this-way-or-that-way situations that you got to study out. That lady and me, it's clear we're running on different tracks, and no switches open between 'em. What she's got to offer, that could have been tempting. But then I'd have been Mr. Mrs. Sutcliff around here, and I don't see myself just that way. So I'm the tumbleweed in her life, and about to be on my way. And the cabbage she talked of . . . that'd be the late Sutcliff.

Then what the fuck did she mean about the loco weed?

Cole Herkimer snapped him out of a deep sleep with a pre-dawn drumbeat on the room's door.

"Maxwell has been found in a gulch with his throat cut," the marshal said, his face stern. "Would you have any ideas about it?"

"Sure not." Faro began pulling on his clothes, yawning and trying to collect his thoughts. Where the hell were those diamonds now? He could feel some kind of suspicion coming from Herkimer. Only why? Did he know that the diamonds had been in Faro's room?

"The suspicion," said Herkimer, and Faro almost jumped at the word, "points to McCluskie."

"But McCluskie has been in your jail this good while," Faro said.

"Maxwell must have been murdered a couple of days back. You can see by the condition of the body."

"And the diamonds?"

"Not a sign of 'em."

Faro said, "I was with Henry about three nights ago, I can figure it out when I get time to think, get some coffee in me. Yes, about three nights. It was, in fact, three nights."

"I'll have to check with Doc Grimsman about the exact time of death," Herkimer said. And he left saying, "In which case I will need you as a witness."

Chapter 13

In preparation for his big game with "You Lose" Lewis that night Faro made his way to the bank. Evelyn was not there, and he had to deal with the clerk. But the withdrawal went off easily. In the back of his mind was not only the thought that he would need a hefty bankroll for the game, but also that if the Maxwell diamonds situation got out of hand a swift getaway would be clearly indicated. Thus, he withdrew his entire deposit.

For clearly someone was, or at least had been, trying to frame him. Why else were the diamonds put in his room like that? But why frame him? He had absolutely no idea. Yet, the evidence was clear, and he was beginning to get mad over it. Dammit, one thing Faro Blake had never cottoned to was anyone trying to use him in any way whatsoever.

Just as he was walking up Main Street from the bank he bumped into the marshal. For the first time since he had known him, Cole Herkimer had a worried look on his face.

"Just heard some bad news, Blake."

"Which is?"

"The Texans, Maxwell's trail crew. They didn't favor Maxwell all that much; fact, some of them hated the bastard. But they are still really pissed at what happened. Like him or not, what they're looking at is that it isn't right to allow your boss to get himself murdered by some damn Yankee."

"I can understand their point," Faro agreed. "And I see yours. They're on the prod unless you come up with the killer."

"And pronto."

"What will they do?"

"They will tree the town, and then take it apart board by board."

"So what are you going to do?" Faro knew what was coming.

"I need deputies, Blake."

"You need an army."

Herkimer nodded.

"How much time do you have?" Faro had no wish to get involved in the town's policing or its politics. But he knew he had to go carefully, for it was plain now that Herkimer had him under suspicion. Lately, and especially right now, there was something distinctly different in the marshal's manner toward him.

Herkimer looked at the sky, squinting. He put his hands in the pockets of his fine California trousers, and extending his right leg, he raised his toe and dropping his head studied it, his chin almost on his chest.

"They will bring the herd in tomorrow or day after. As soon as they sell their critters they're saying they want the killer of Hobart Maxwell."

Faro let a little whistle escape between his pursed lips.

"I am still needing deputies," Herkimer said.

"Let me think it over, Marshal."

Herkimer suddenly cut his eye to the bank from which he had obviously seen Faro emerge. "You are not leaving town, are you?"

"Just a visit to the bank, Marshal. I've got a big game coming up with Hughie Lewis. I'm going to need all my cash." And with a remark about the weather he took his departure. In spite of all the trouble he felt gathering around him, he was looking forward to the game with "You Lose" Lewis.

Faro had spent considerable time that very morning in preparation for the game with Lewis. It was not that "You Lose" was such hot shakes as a poker player—far from it. But Faro was a professional, a perfectionist, and he believed in serious training for his work.

Faro had learned early in life that a sound poker player could win *any* poker game. But what made a "sound" poker player?

"Never," A.B. had told him emphatically, "never in deuces wild stay with one wild card unless you hold three jacks or better." Faro remembered this as he walked toward the Goldroom and the rendezvous with "You Lose" for he was intending to deal five-card draw with deuces wild. Yes, he reflected, a sound poker player only stayed in a game he knew he was going to win. The sound player folded, the weak player hung in there when he didn't have a chance.

He remembered old Cal Kimberley who, after the deal, when his time came to bet, would scratch the side of his long nose. Whenever Cal did this he always bet or raised, and it was certain that he carried a strong hand.

Another cattleman, Homer Fowles, would pretend not to realize it was his turn to bet. Then he would hurriedly light a smoke and bet. And he would not be bluffing; he would have those cards.

Then one, a cattle buyer from K.C.—what the hell was his name? Ah yes, Childs, Shanghai Childs, could never keep his hands from shaking when he was going for a big one.

And there were the conversational players, and those who would drum their fingers, or those who would smile when their hand was helped. And those who could not control their voices. Listening with a very fine alertness, Faro could catch the change in voice, the inflection, the emphasis, which told him which way that player was going.

Ah, it was fun. It was great fun, the details, the little unnoticed moments; except he would notice them, and they revealed everything. It was what made the game so damned exciting.

"You Lose" had evidently been delayed, and so Faro used the time by watching a game in progress. There were seven players, and he soon noticed that four of them consistently stayed. From this he realized that the game was not tight because that many players out of a game of seven had no chance of maintaining a minimum power. The only thing to figure then was that there were a few weak players. He was in the process of developing this observation when "You Lose" Lewis walked in.

"What's this I hear about some Texan getting his throat cut?"

Faro told him about Hobart Maxwell and his diamonds, leaving out his own implication in the affair, however.

"You Lose" looked bonier than ever. His long, lean jaws framed a mouthful of brown teeth in the center of which were two spaces, upper and lower. When under the influence of what "You Lose" always referred to as his "favorite beverage," whiskey with beer chaser, "You Lose" would squirt beer at any target for a bet. On one or two occasions this funning of his had led to a near passage-at-arms when the selected target happened to be another human. But everyone loved "You Lose," and so feelings were stroked, tempers mollified and the damage paid for by that big Texas heart.

"You Lose" would bet on anything. Anything. One of his most famous bets involved a fellow Texan who had deposited his life savings in a San Francisco bank only to discover one day that the bank was bankrupt. "You Lose" had been out drinking with his friend the night before, and the shock of the news brought the two of them to instant sobriety. But "You Lose's" friend was resourceful. He was not named Stonehead Harrigan for nothing. "That goddam bank has an office in Portland, Oregon," he told "You Lose."

"What do you mean by that?" "You Lose" had asked.

"Simple. Portland is almost seven hundred miles from Frisco. They won't have this news of the bank failure till they get it from the steamer. I get me a fast horse or two and I, by God, can make it." And Stonehead was on his way.

"You Lose," in telling the story, always mentioned how shocked he was to discover that Stonehead really was a stone head. But he was his friend, and "You Lose" loved to bet. Immediately, he rounded up some betting acquaintances and laid his money on Stonehead Harrigan beating the steamer to Portland.

"What happened?" Faro, just like everyone else, had asked "You Lose" when he first heard the oft-told story.

"You Lose," as he always did, grinned all over his face, revealing both wide gaps in his upper and lower teeth.

"Stonehead made it, by God! He made it, about a half hour before the steamer docked with the news of the bank failure, and he got his money out on time."

"He was an enterprising young fellow," Faro allowed.

"Young, my ass!" roared "You Lose." "Harrigan was sixty-five in the shade, by God, and he rode his ass off gettin' to Portland in time. And I always thinks of him when I got me a big bet going. Hell, Stonehead won me a packet with that ride of his."

The game at hand progressed as usual—some winning, some losing. Faro was playing carefully. The man opposite him looked bored. The man on his left dozed between hands, his lids closed tight, his head bobbing a little. Harvey Golightly, a government man, was getting some good hands and was winning fairly consistently. The other two were holding their own, and so was "You Lose."

At one point Faro got up to stretch his legs. For some reason or other he had a feeling that something was going to go wrong.

Tod Varney, a red-faced man with very red hands and a red neck was fumbling with the deck. He had put in the joker preparatory to dealing deuces wild and was awkwardly reshuffling the cards.

"You Lose" Lewis watched him in disgust. "Goddamit, Varney, either shit or get off the pot."

Startled, Varney said, "Hold your vinegar." And he continued to take his time.

A man named Henderson bet, studying his cards first under the brim of his big stetson hat. Clyde Wood folded, and Griswold, a drummer, tossed his hand into the discards in disgust.

But "You Lose" was grinning impishly now. "I raise one hundred," he said and tossed in his chips.

Faro, who only bet on a strong hand, threw his hand in the discards, as did Varney.

Harvey Golightly looked over at Henderson. "I up you five hundred," he said. And Faro could tell he had them. Golightly smiled as Henderson called, and Harvey raked in the pot with four queens.

The game had suddenly come to life, and now there was a big crowd standing around the table. Faro noted that Cole Herkimer was one of those present. On the next hand the betting started slowly, but then built up to where there was ten thousand dollars in the pot, and Faro was debating with himself whether to let Lewis bluff him out of it so he could set up the Texan for a major take later on, or whether to go for it.

He was hot; indeed, so was everyone else, for as usual no one had thought to open a window. The air in the room was thick and sticky, and when someone brushed close to Faro, he felt an instant annoyance. It was hot enough without the crowd moving in so close, dammit.

Facing "You Lose" Lewis across the table, he had about decided to let the Texan take it, so that he could clobber him later. Stalling for time, to let the moment build, he took out his handkerchief to mop his brow. Something made a little thump on the baize top of the round table, and looking down, Faro saw to his utter amazement and massive dismay that it was a diamond. There was no question but that it had come from his own pocket. There was no question whose diamond it was. And there was for sure no question that he was in big trouble.

Chapter 14

The Honeytown jail was nothing to write home about. It was not, as is said, well-appointed. A single cell—at present occupied by the recuperating Horrible Henry McCluskie—a small area in front of it, a window and a door leading to the marshal's office made up the architecture of Honeytown's detention quarters.

On the way over from the Goldroom to Herkimer's office Faro related the complete story of the diamonds: how he had discovered them in his case and had hidden them in the bottle of bourbon, and how they had since disappeared.

"Someone is trying to frame me," he told Herkimer. "Why? I just don't know. But whoever it is, it's got to be the original thief, and more than likely the man who killed Maxwell."

"Blake, I'm inclined to believe you. The only thing is I have got to lock you up for your own

139

protection at the very least. Maxwell's trail crew will have got the news by now, about that diamond being in your possession, and they'll be looking to string you up. Also, there is the question of where the rest of the diamonds are."

"I sure wish I knew."

Herkimer shrugged. "In fact, if all you get out of this is a necktie party you'll be lucky. And that is a gut." Herkimer was striding along fast, with Faro right close to him, and now the marshal suddenly stopped short, Faro almost bumping into him. "They might even take it in mind to hit the jail, and I would have to hide you someplace. Hell, man, a mob is a real ugly thing."

It was all there, Faro realized as the cell door clanged shut behind him. The next sound he heard was Horrible Henry's deep chuckle.

"Welcome to Honeytown Hotel." The giant was lying supine on his back on one of the cell's two bunks. This unfortunate piece of furniture was groaning under its enormous burden, the center of the bed almost touching the floor, the legs splayed like a riled bronc ready to give up or try one more buck, as Henry continued to chuckle, sending more shocks and quivers through the weakening structure.

Horrible was smoking a cigar, which, Faro judged, was made of rope soaked in tar and sheep dip.

"You look sick as a tomcat about to get it," Faro said sardonically.

"I am in good shape," allowed Horrible Henry, "considerin'. But you don't look none too sparky, Mister Gambler Blake." And he chuckled again while the bed all but collapsed.

Faro sat down on the edge of the bunk across from McCluskie and let a long sigh run all the way through his body.

It was no place to be. That was for sure. Those lively, ornery Texans would sooner than later be putting in an appearance, and Faro knew they would be in no mood for reasoned discussion or debate. Only, who had killed Hobart Maxwell? Who had robbed the Texan in the first place?

Faro had been lying on his bunk for about an hour trying to see his way through the puzzle when Herkimer returned. Horrible Henry, meanwhile, had been snoring like a drunken longhorn, making sleep for Faro totally impossible.

The marshal had brought Faro's traveling grip and his gambling-tools case from the Chicago House. These he placed on the table outside the cell and deftly went through the contents, pausing with amusement at the holdouts and other rigging in the tool case. Finally, he let Faro out of the cell and frisked him. He kept the Reid and the roll of twenty thousand dollars which Faro had withdrawn from the bank.

Pocketing the Reid knuckle-duster, he said conversationally, "Handy little weapon. And this will be in the safe." He held up the roll of bank notes, then added, "Minus this." And he began counting off a sizable amount of bills.

"What the hell are you doing!" Faro stared at him incredulously.

"Thass his fee," roared Horrible Henry from the cell behind him. "You didn't think our honest and upright marshal was living on any itty-bitty two-fifty a month did ya?"

And now suddenly it was a quite different Cole Herkimer standing in front of him, Faro saw. A Cole Herkimer who was all ice. It fit, by God, it did sure fit.

Herkimer watched him getting it with an amused smile at the corners of his mouth.

"I told you it was no easy job being marshal in this town, Blake."

"So you greased it."

"But of course. Wouldn't you?"

"And you had a good teacher."

"The best."

"Except where is he now?"

"Mister Henry Plummer. Sheriff of Bannack and Virginia City," roared Horrible Henry, getting to his feet and gripping the bars on the cell door. "Plummer—thass his teacher. An' mine too." He broke into spasmodic laughter, moving his jaws around as though chewing vigorously on the words and laughter too. "And Whiskey Bill and Dutch Smith and Bummer Howe . . . we had a real good one goin'. 'Course that was just a few of the boys. Shit, we had a whole army like. Not to mention Mister Crawford Hinds! You can figure how come our honest and upright marshal didn't want to pull in poor old Crawford."

"Ah, I see," said Faro. And then you graduated to here."

"I did," Herkimer said, cold. "This fool had to follow."

"So he was always a threat. He could talk."

"Always a threat," agreed Herkimer. "But soon he won't be. Nor will you."

"I see you really learned a lot from Plummer."

"Rode with him," Herkimer said, and Faro

thought he heard a note of admiration in the words. "Knee to britches."

"Exceptin' you didn't swing with him," cut in Horrible Henry. "Too bad."

"Too bad for you," Herkimer said with a cold smile.

"Ole King Cole let the vigilantes swing poor Henry by hisself along with Ives and Red Yaeger and the rest." McCluskie belched suddenly and loudly. There was a big grin on his face as he said, "We could make a deal with you, Cole."

"No deal."

"Whyn't you listen? I'm talking about the Texans taking this town. You think they'll stop at Blake?" He spat with sudden anger on the cell floor, getting some of it on the bars. "Shit man, they'll just as lief take us all. You know how mobs are." He paused, seeing that Herkimer was listening. "What I'm sayin' is, you want to come out lily white in this action, get off scot-free, then hire me an' Blake as deppities, an' we'll be two good guns sidin' ya."

"So you could hightail it, huh?" Herkimer sneered. "I am not doing any such foolish thing, Henry. And for now I am sticking close to both of you, closer than a tick to a longhorn in spring-time."

"Marshal, you know you have got to treat me nice," Horrible insisted. "I mean, like I could get conversational."

"Who to? To Blake?" An icy laugh fell from Herkimer's lips as he pocketed the bills he had peeled off Faro's bankroll. "The rest will be in the safe," he said as he put one roll in his trouser pocket and the other in the pocket of his coat. He broke out laughing.

And Horrible Henry roared with mirth. "By God, Blake, Cole has a real humor, you have got to admit!"

"Back into the cell, Blake," Cole said, and his voice was real cold. The marshal had his hand close to his six-gun as he spoke.

Faro was not at all happy over the way the conversation had turned, for the more that Herkimer was revealed, the less chance he had of getting out of Honeytown alive. And that final gesture of the marshal's—taking all his money—just about settled it. The cell door clanging behind him was like doom.

"Reckon that be it, Blake," McCluskie said when Herkimer walked back into his office. "He will get us one way or t'other; kill us straight out and claim we wuz makin' a break for it, or he'll let the Texans do it."

"Shit," said Faro.

"And two is eight," added Horrible, and he was not now laughing.

"That is right," Herkimer said, coming back into the hallway outside the cell, having overheard them. "I will either fail, valiantly, at saving you boys from that desperate Texas cowboy mob or I will be forced to kill you while you try to escape." He spread his hands, and his face and eyes were quite without any expression at all.

"You sonofabitch," Faro said.

"Thank you," said Cole Herkimer with a little bow. He had his right hand on his gun now as he stepped forward and, with his left, placed the key in the lock of the cell door. "The difference between us, of course, will be one of mobility. That's to say, I will be a live sonofabitch, but you . . . you will be a dead one." And he swung the door open, the Deane & Adams out of its holster now. He motioned with the gun. "Faro Blake first," he said.

"I want to know one thing," Faro said, trying to keep his voice level.

"And that is?"

"Why you framed me. Why me? In fact, why was it necessary to frame anybody?"

Cole Herkimer's thin lips twisted in a sneer. "I thought Maxwell was dead. A mistake. But I was afraid he might have seen me when I shot him off his horse. So I had to get rid of those diamonds—fast—but in a place where I could either get them again or let them be found; I mean a place, a situation I could control."

"Why did you kill him finally?"

"He was telling everyone he'd seen who shot him and was just waiting for his memory to return. I couldn't take the chance that he might point at me."

Herkimer had locked the cell door behind Faro. Only the two of them were in the little hallway. He motioned with the gun now for Faro to move over to the wall.

Faro, wildly racking his brain to find a way out, could find nothing. Could he distract Herkimer? Was there a way to use McCluskie? But nothing came. And he could feel the sweat pouring down his face and neck and down his back and chest.

"I see you ain't choosin' to wait for the Texans," Henry said from the cell.

"Took you some piece of time to figure that out, didn't it?" And a mirthless smile touched the marshal's lips.

"But," Faro insisted in a louder voice, trying one last stab at it. "But why *me*? Why did you frame *me*? It couldn't have been just because I happened to be handy." He had still not turned to face the wall as Herkimer had ordered, but remained facing the marshal with his arms down at his sides.

Herkimer looked at him over his six-gun. Now, all at once, his face had gone very white. The blue eyes seemed to glitter. His mouth was a slash in his blank face. Indeed, he was not even in his face, Faro suddenly realized, but behind it somewhere. Faro watched the hatred stare out through that chalk white mask.

"Why?" he said. And the voice sounded as Faro had never heard it before. "Why, Blake? I will tell you why." And Faro felt he was looking at a skull.

"Yes, Blake, I will tell you why," he repeated, gripping the revolver, and for a moment Faro feared he was going to pull the trigger. But Herkimer controlled himself. "Why? Why, because I was in the closet."

"Closet? What closet? What the hell—"

"The night you came back, you bastard. I heard it all. You and our charming hostess." The words were a hiss as his mouth worked, and he could barely get his breath. His lips were dry as paper. "And you are going to die, Blake, you are going to die."

And at that moment Faro knew he was going to win.

"So you were her lover."

"I was indeed."

"And were you not also business partners?" And when Herkimer said nothing he went on.

"Didn't she give you tips on the investors and depositors in Honeytown—who had what and where—so that you and your gang could know where to make a juicy hit?" He paused; he had him. "That's what she told me, Herkimer. And she told me how she used to get some of that information. Not only from the bank business records . . . but on her back."

Herkimer began to shake. Faro was gambling that his anger and jealousy would make an opening. But if he went too far Herkimer might shoot.

Now Faro played his ace. "She told me something about you, you know."

He watched the other man's face turn gray.

"She told me how you couldn't get it up."

Cole Herkimer's eyes were like bullets. A long moment passed, and Faro could hear his own heart pounding as the sweat rolled down him.

Suddenly Herkimer holstered his gun. In a flash he had drawn a skinning knife. "Shooting is too good for you, you fucking swine." He began moving in a sort of half circle in front of Faro.

Faro swiftly loosened his coat and moved away from the spot where he had been standing. As he did so he felt the deck of new cards in his waistcoat pocket. Swiftly he took them out and broke open the pack.

"This is no time for a card game, you fool."

But Faro wasn't about to deal a hand. He suddenly threw the whole deck into Herkimer's face, letting it fan out—except for one card which he held in his right hand. Now, as the marshal moved in reaction, Faro ducked, brought the heel of his left hand against the wrist holding the skinning knife and with the edge of the hard, brand-new playing card slashed Herkimer across his eyes.

Herkimer let out a scream of pain and surprise, while Faro now brought his boot right into his crotch, and followed with a tremendous blow along the side of Herkimer's jugular vein. The marshal dropped to the floor.

But he was a tough one. While the still-imprisoned Horrible Henry cheered, Herkimer rolled to his feet and now he had his gun in his hand, covering Faro.

He could hardly see from the slash Faro's card had given him. Wiping the blood from his eyes he snarled, "It'll be the gun for sure, Blake, and this what you have done will only strengthen my position, while you tried your jail break."

But his vision, Faro could see, was badly blurred. And as he raised the Deane & Adams to fire, Faro dodged to the side. Yet Herkimer shook his head and still covered his prisoner.

"You almost had me, Blake. Jealousy is a true devil, I will agree. But we shall not allow it to interfere with our business at hand. I have my stake and by morning I will be long gone. And you will be dead."

"Gone with the diamonds I presume," said Faro, still fighting for time.

Herkimer wiped the blood from his face, making a ghastly smear. "With the diamonds and with your kind personal contribution I shall manage quite well." He lifted the six-gun.

"Where are the diamonds?" Faro asked quickly. "Where did you hide them?"

"In a safe place, Blake. They are oh so well

hidden this time. You would never guess in a million years."

"Then I think you had better tell me where they are," a voice behind him said suddenly as Evelyn Sutcliff walked through the door that led to the outer office. She was carrying a shotgun, and it was pointed right at Cole Herkimer. "Drop that revolver, Cole. And tell me where the diamonds are." Her eyes glittered. "I have heard it all, you fool; I have been here for at least ten minutes. You didn't really believe you could get away with running out on me, with double-crossing me!"

Chapter 15

Evelyn Sutcliff stood furious and beautiful in front of Cole Herkimer with that deadly-looking shotgun pointed right at his belly.

"Long gone? You say you'll be long gone, Cole Herkimer?"

"I didn't mean that, Evelyn." Herkimer's words were soft with the lie. And again Faro saw yet another Herkimer. Herkimer the jealous, frustrated lover mixed with Herkimer the man of greed and, yes, insecurity.

"You damn fool!" Evelyn's eyes flashed; her cheeks were alive with color. She tossed her head. "You fool! You say you heard me and him, that you were in the bedroom closet that night." She shook her head again, her voice breaking with scorn. "Don't you realize I knew you were there all along?"

Herkimer looked as though he had been struck

dumb. And Faro was a bit shaken by the revelation, too. This place, a little voice kept telling him, was no place to be.

After a moment, Herkimer managed to blurt out, "What . . . what are you saying?"

"I am saying that I *knew* you were there in the bedroom closet. I heard you sneaking back before Blake got there, so I made damned sure you'd have plenty to hear." She lowered the shotgun. "I wanted to make you jealous. Because you are such an arrogant swine. And now, now you speak of being long gone."

She stood there shaking her head from side to side. "No. No. Never! You are not going to leave me here, Cole Herkimer. Not here, not in Honeytown. I want my chance for happiness too. I want those diamonds and the good life. It's because of me you even heard of the diamonds in the first place. I want to travel. I want to live." She took a step forward. "I wanted that with you. But you . . . you fucking bastard!" Suddenly she raised the shotgun. Tears were pouring out of her eyes and down her cheeks.

"Don't, Evelyn!" Herkimer took a step toward her, horror in his voice. She was pointing the twin barrels of the shotgun right at him.

"For God's sake, Evelyn, don't shoot. Dear God, don't shoot! We'll go away together. We'll share the diamonds." Herkimer was all but falling to his knees in supplication as he moved toward Evelyn, his hands outstretched.

"Evelyn, we'll go away. Oh yes, we'll be together. See, I was only trying to make you jealous. See, I knew you were there in the office just now." He suddenly gave a ghastly laugh as her finger curled on the trigger. "I knew you were there listening all along. Yes I did. And I, too, wanted you to want me more. Oh, don't shoot. Don't shoot!"

"You lying swine!"

He had almost reached her and, in fact, had his hand just on the barrel of the twelve-gauge when a blast tore into the room, all but deafening Faro and Horrible Henry both, and carrying Cole Herkimer like a torn rag to the floor.

Faro did not hesitate. With a bound he had covered the distance between himself and Evelyn and while she stood staring in horror at what her rage had just done, he brought his fist under her jaw, knocking her out cold. It was the first time he had ever hit a woman in his life, but it was also the first time he had ever been that close to death at the hands of a woman.

Who knew what such a crazed person might do under such circumstances. She could as easily turn the gun on him and Horrible Henry, or on herself, for the second load of shot. He checked quickly to see that she was out—but not badly damaged—and would be all right. Then he picked up the shotgun and, kneeling beside Herkimer, quickly went through his pockets, retrieving his money and his Reid knuckle-duster. Herkimer was a mass of blood; and sure dead.

There was nothing else of importance on the marshal's body but a dozen shotgun shells in his coat pocket. Suddenly Faro bent closer. There was something strange about those wounds. They were not what one would have expected from a blast of shot at close range; they were far fewer and smaller, albeit the load had been fatal. Faro studied them, puzzled, and now he found himself all at once attracted by something glinting in the wall behind Herkimer.

"Blake, let's haul ass," cried Horrible Henry. "Let me outta this tin can. Shit, what the hell you starin' at! Can't you hear them Texans down the street. They have got the news for sure!"

Ignoring Horrible Henry, Faro crossed the little hall and began to dig out a tiny fragment of something like glass that was stuck in the wall. He held it up to the light, watching its glitter. Struck by a sudden thought, he drew the piece across the crystal of his pocket watch. It left a scratch.

Still paying no mind to Horrible Henry, he took one of the shotgun shells that had been in Herkimer's pocket and opened it.

His head reeled then. For instead of the load of shot, there was a diamond. So that was the hiding place. No wonder Herkimer had been so horrified, so pleading for mercy, for to him worse than being shot was the horrible thought of those precious stones being shattered.

Swift as a whip Faro grabbed up the shotgun shells and pocketed them, not overlooking the second shell in the shotgun. Horrible Henry, bent only on escape, had realized nothing of the discovery.

"Blake, for Chrissake, let's git on and git out! I want shut of this place!"

Swiftly, Faro unlocked the cell, and the two of them swept into the office. But they could hear the Texans outside.

"There's a back way, up through the roof," said Horrible. "Follow me."

And he quickly led the way to the rear of the building, even as they could hear shots hitting the lock on the front door.

In a trice they were on the roof and crossing swiftly to a second, then a third building; then they dropped to the alley that opened onto a back street.

"We'll cut to the livery," Horrible said, gasping for breath from his exertions.

"Not me. We'll split here," Faro said. He held out his hand. "Been nice knowing you," he said, real wry. And before Horrible Henry could say anything, he had turned on his heel and was racing down the back street.

He knew it was out of the question that he could make a getaway on a horse with those wild Texans behind him. Of course, they might have the good sense to revive Evelyn Sutcliff and get the straight of things from her. But then they might not.

Faro didn't give it another thought as he raced through the back alleys of Honeytown just as dawn was breaking. He could only hope he was playing it right. It was something he was pretty sure he had heard "You Lose" Lewis say when they had been in the Chicago House. It was something that he just prayed was right.

Chapter 16

Hughie "You Lose" Lewis was sitting glumly in his private railroad car as the early morning train pulled out of the Honeytown yards. He felt irritated. The game with Blake, to which he'd been looking forward for so long, had just been going nicely when there was all that damn foofaraw over some damn diamond. He never did get the straight of it after that asshole marshal had taken Blake to the pokey.

Lewis's luck, it was. Always the same. And he could have made a real killing. He knew it; he knew it sure as he knew God made little apples and big ones. More important, he would have gone up against the great Faro Blake and come out ahead. Shit! Because now it looked like it would be this real good while before he'd get a chance to lock horns with Blake again. And he began to wonder idly if maybe even Faro had felt he was going to lose big and had been in cahoots with the marshal to bail him out of it. But "You Lose" let that one pass from his mind.

As the train began to move a little faster, he heard something hitting on the side of the car outside. Looking out the window he saw a man running beside the train. By God!

"You Lose" lowered the window and just as the train took on more speed he hauled Faro Blake into the car.

"Glad you could drop in," said "You Lose."

"Sorry about the little interruption last night," replied Faro taking out a deck of cards. "Shall we continue where we left off?"

"You Lose" smiled. And Faro grinned. One thing he liked about westerners was that they seldom asked you any embarrassing questions.

And one thing he liked about "You Lose" Lewis was that he had a lot of money. What with the Maxwell diamonds, his own stake, and "You Lose's" bankroll—which he would surely win— Faro knew he was going to be sitting pretty.

WESTERNS THAT NEVER DIE

They pack excitement that lasts a lifetime.
It's no wonder Zane Grey is the bestselling
Western writer of all time.
Get these Zane Grey Western adventures
from Pocket Books:

————	83102	BORDER LEGION $1.75
————	82896	BOULDER DAM $1.75
————	83422	RIDERS OF THE PURPLE SAGE $1.95
————	82692	DEER STALKER $1.75
————	82883	KNIGHTS OF THE RANGE $1.75
————	82878	ROBBERS ROOST $1.75
————	82076	TO THE LAST MAN $1.75
————	83534	UNDER THE TONTO RIM $1.95
————	82880	U.P. TRAIL $1.75
————	83022	ARIZONA CLAN $1.75
————	83105	BLACK MESA $1.75
————	83309	CALL OF THE CANYON $1.75